MW00908758

WHAT
TOMORROW
BRINGS

WHAT TOMORROW BRINGS

PAGE MASON

ARCHWAY
PUBLISHING

Copyright © 2014 Alison Schriver.

All rights reserved. No part of this book may be used or reproduced by any means, graphic, electronic, or mechanical, including photocopying, recording, taping or by any information storage retrieval system without the written permission of the publisher except in the case of brief quotations embodied in critical articles and reviews.

Archway Publishing books may be ordered through booksellers or by contacting:

Archway Publishing
1663 Liberty Drive
Bloomington, IN 47403
www.archwaypublishing.com
1-(888)-242-5904

Because of the dynamic nature of the Internet, any web addresses or links contained in this book may have changed since publication and may no longer be valid. The views expressed in this work are solely those of the author and do not necessarily reflect the views of the publisher, and the publisher hereby disclaims any responsibility for them.

Any people depicted in stock imagery provided by Thinkstock are models, and such images are being used for illustrative purposes only. Certain stock imagery © Thinkstock.

ISBN: 978-1-4808-1219-2 (sc)
ISBN: 978-1-4808-1220-8 (e)

Library of Congress Control Number: 2014918253

Printed in the United States of America.

Archway Publishing rev. date: 10/30/2014

Dedication

Thank you to my friends and family for your support, editing, reading, and ideas throughout this process. I could not have done it without any of you. Thank you to my students for reminding me to keep trying. Chase your dreams!

Prologue

The sky was gray and the dim room had baskets of flowers and plants scattered on any flat surface that could be found. The walls had pictures of smiling faces and lively landscapes, but the room was void of any happiness. Sympathy cards were piled on the table by the front door with keys and loose change. The oversized chair was next to the front window where a 43 year old woman was just realizing that she was a widow.

Amanda had been married for 20 years to her high school sweetheart. Todd was a great man, father and husband. Five days ago he went for a bike ride through the park. As he was returning home, he had a heart attack and veered of the bike trail into a tree. He died instantly. Amanda's world was shattered in that instant. Her 18 year old son was getting ready to start his senior year in high school and she was alone in the house that she and Todd built into a lovely home.

"Amanda, do you want something to eat, drink?" Her mother's sympathetic eyes rested on the shell of a woman sitting in the chair. Donna walked over and wrapped the afghan around Amanda's drooped shoulders.

Amanda gazed at her mother and slightly shook her head. She was trying to figure out what to do next. *How am I going to go on? Todd was the rock and I can't do this alone. Brett needs his father. I know nothing about being a young man. What am I going to do?*

The clouds continued to block out the sun, the gloom was also within this woman. What was to come of her and her son?

1

Two Years Later

Amanda walked through the beige, block hallway and smiled. Summer break was finally here. The students were chatting excitedly about swimming and going to the beach. Their excitement helped Amanda feel eager to go into the June sun and start her summer vacation.

Brett would be home from school tonight. He had finished his freshman year at Temple. He was ready for the break from academics. Amanda was not sure when he would start working his summer job with the nursery but she looked forward to spending time with him. The house was lonely without him. Amanda packed some last minute things into her school bag and heard the buzzing of her phone. She pulled it from the pocket; Brett's face was on the screen.

"Hey you!"

"Hi Mom! I'm home!"

Amanda smiled and sighed, "I'm so glad. I'm leaving school now. I will see you in fifteen."

"Ok, see you."

She flipped the ringer back on and tucked her phone in the pocket. Carefully she slid the straps onto her shoulder and turned toward the door. The lights were off and with one more glance into the classroom she closed the door.

The drive home was quick and familiar. Amanda was glad she decided to stay in the house after Todd died. It was the only home Brett had ever known and having memories of Todd helped her cope with the loss. As the radio played the latest Taylor Swift song, Amanda smiled and remembered when she and Todd first brought Brett home from the hospital. It seemed like a lifetime ago but the memory was clear and fond. The car came to the top of the hill and Brett's Subaru was in the driveway. Amanda pulled into the garage and hurriedly grabbed her stuff and ran in the kitchen door. Brett was talking on his cell looking out into the backyard. He turned when heard her and held his free arm out for her. She slipped under his arm and squeezed him. *Boy, I've missed him.*

"Wow! You're strong." Brett said winking at her after ending the call.

Amanda playfully punched him, "That's right I am. I can take you and I am not that old." They both laughed and hugged again. Amanda felt happy and safe with her son home. Brett looked and sounded so much like his dad. It was like he was still in the house when he is home. Her heart warmed and broke a little at the same time.

"Whatcha ya doing tonight, Mom? I was going to see the guys tonight. Is that ok? Did you have plans?"

"No Honey! Go hang with the boys. Please be careful and call me if you need anything. I have to call Stephanie. She called about meeting her in New York. By the way… I'm *so* glad you're home. I've missed you!"

"I've missed you too. The guys wanna get pizza and go back to Scott's house. I'll call if I'm going to be late. You sure it's ok?"

"Yes! Please go be with your friends. Maybe brunch tomorrow?"

"You bet. Thanks Mom. I'll see you later!" Brett grabbed his keys from the table by the door and came back to the kitchen to give Amanda a quick kiss on the check.

Amanda watched and smiled proudly at her son. *What a young man he had become. Todd would be so proud. What did I need to do tonight? Oh, yeah! Call Stephanie!*

The phone rang four times, Stephanie picked up. Pots were banging, voices giggling and music playing. Amanda hoped she wasn't interrupting. She knew that the kids and Stephanie's job kept her pretty busy and she didn't want to add to her crazy everyday life.

"Hey, Stephie! What's going on?"

"Hi Mandy!"

Amanda winced. Mandy was the nickname she would've loved to have left in elementary school.

"I was wondering if you'd like to come to a picnic in the Hamptons in two weeks. I cleared it with Doug to have the kids and I could meet you at the train station and we could leave from here. Please say you will come! *Please!*"

Amanda smiled fondly at the pleading, "Of course. I'll say something to Brett, but it shouldn't be a problem." Stephanie worked for a publishing company, so events like this sometimes included authors, editors and other publishers.

"Well… we'd meet with some writers, actors and movie producers. I'm thinkin' girls' weekend in the Hamptons. Whatcha you think? Can you?"

"Yes!" Amanda was trying to keep from laughing. "I'll get my train ticket. When do you want me?"

"Try to get the afternoon train two Thursdays from now. Text me when you have your arrival time. Thanks Mandy! I am so glad you're willing to come!"

"I might change my mind if you don't stop calling me Mandy." Amanda teased. "Promise not to call me Mandy, and I will come." Her smile was serious tone she was trying to keep.

"Alright, alright! I will call you Amanda. Sorry!" faking her exasperation.

A crash came vibrating through the phone. "Steph, is everything alright?"

"*Ryan*! Get out of the closet! You are making a mess!" Stephanie screamed past the handset. "Sorry Mand...Amanda! I have to go. The boys are knocking things everywhere. I will talk to you soon. Kiss kiss!"

"Bye honey." Amanda gently placed the phone on the table and thought about what to eat for dinner. A bowl of cereal sounded perfect. The bowl in her hand and the TV chattering about some new movie or show, Amanda was relaxing and thinking about how relaxing the beach will be. It would be a great getaway with Stephanie. They don't get to spend much time together since their lives are busy. It has been a lifelong friendship that has been through her divorce, death of parents, birth of children and watching them grow up. No matter how long they went without talking to each other, they could pick up the conversation right where they left off. It was a wonderful relationship that Amanda treasured.

~ℓↄ~

The house felt like a home again, full of life and laughter even though, Brett was working at the nursery and then helping around the house. Amanda spent time cleaning and organizing all the things that she is too busy to take care of during the school year. He told Amanda he might have Scott come over and play video games and eat pizza. Amanda felt safe and comforted knowing Scott was coming over. They had been friends forever and didn't get to spend time together. Scott lived at home and worked full time and didn't go to college. His mom got sick his senior year of high school and he needed to stay home and help take care of his brother and sister. Brett thought of him as the brother he never had and liked doing guy stuff with Scott when he was home.

~ᴕᴑᴦ~

"Brett! Where's my train ticket? I printed it and I can't find it."

"Mom, you laid it on the table by the door with your phone right on top of it. Would you relax! You're going to have fun and enjoy yourself. I'll be fine. It's all good."

Amanda smiled and messed his hair as she passed him sitting at the kitchen table. "I'm not worried about you."

"Mom, you'll have a blast. Enjoy the break."

"Thanks Buddy! I'll try."

"Are you ready to go to the train station?" he asked winking at her.

She nodded and gathered her bags. Brett took the suitcase and kissed her cheek. The ride was short and painless but parking was limited.

"Don't park. Let me out here. Thanks honey for driving. I'll call you to let you know when to pick me up. Ok?"

"Sounds good! Call if you need anything. Love you!" Brett handed her the suitcase and squeezes her in a hug.

"Love you, too. I'm so lucky to have such a good boy. Take care and have fun. You know where I am if you need me." Amanda pulled out of the hug and turned quickly away so Brett wouldn't see the tears in her eyes. It was at moments like this when she wished Todd were here to see how great his son turned out. He nodded and moved back to the driver's seat.

"See you Sunday! Have fun!"

"Bye," Amanda waved and she watched him pull out of the parking lot. She yanked the suitcase and headed up to the platform. Summer weekends meant the train would be full, so she filed into the line forming by the tracks. A wave of warmth passed over her as she waited for the train. Leaving Brett and going with Steph to the Hamptons just felt different, like tomorrow was going to bring something new.

2

$\mathcal{T}$he sound of the train on the tracks had a way of lulling Amanda into a drowsy state. The train pulled into Penn Station. Amanda realized it was time to put her book away and gather her belongings. Her excitement was building as she came up the stairs into the main part of the station. She saw Steph's head bobbing above the crowd.

"Mandy! Amanda! I'm over here!" She was waving an umbrella and smiling from ear to ear. Running toward Amanda with her arms flailing all over, people were turning and watching her and ducking out of her way.

Amanda was giddy from watching her friend approach. *Why I love this goofy woman that is now barreling toward me?* Almost 40 years of knowing her, she was still surprising. Amanda dropped her bag and suitcase opening her arms to Steph. They collided and struggled to get their balance giggling uncontrollably.

"Oh Amanda! I'm so glad you are here. Come on. We have some girl bonding to do, drinks to be had, and vitamin D to be soaked in. Give me that suitcase." Stephanie grabbed the handle and dragged the wheels across the tiled floor. She was still wearing her sleek black, sleeveless work dress and black sling backs, weaving through the crowded station like she was on fire.

Amanda was struggling to keep up with her bag and water bottle in her hand. She was in shape but feeling like she needed to up her workout to keep up with Stephanie. The sun was shining through the buildings and the shadows were dancing all over the sidewalks. The blue sky and white cottony clouds were making Amanda's heart and spirit feel light. What a fantastic day to be in this gorgeous city with a great friend. This was the start to a relaxing girls' weekend. The ladies made it to the car in the parking garage two blocks from the station, both a little out of breath. Amanda was smiling as she slid into the passenger seat of Stephanie's car.

"What on earth are you smiling about?" Stephanie said as she backed out of the space. The car was cool and purring in the shade of the garage.

Amanda turned to Steph and nodded. "I'm so happy to see you and *so* looking forward to hanging with you this weekend!" She rubbed her bare arms and felt the warmth of excitement and happiness take over her body. "I have missed you and can't wait to hear all of your news, soak up the sun, read my book and maybe even partake in glass or two of wine." Amanda took a breath to slow down her excitement. "Thanks for inviting me to share this weekend with you."

Steph reached across the console and rubbed Amanda's knee and squeezed. "You betcha! I'd never invite anyone other than my one and only bestie!"

The drive to the Hamptons was full of conversation, laughing, reminiscing, and just a few tears. The girls were so wrapped up in each other's words and thoughts that when they pulled in front of the house, they didn't even realize they had arrived. The GPS saying "You have arrived," pulled them from the bonding.

"We're here! Let me park the car and we can check out the house and our rooms." Stephanie chirped as she glided the car under the car port. She hopped out of the car and popped the trunk. Amanda met her at the trunk and grabbed her suitcase. Both girls skipped toward the front door.

"You're finally here!" They both heard as the front door burst open. Stephanie's colleague, an editor from the office, was smiling at them both with a glass of wine in her hand.

"Hi Grace! We are here and ready to join you in a glass. You have more?"

"Of course! Get in here ladies! I'll show you your rooms and then we can meet in the family room. Good?"

"Perfect!" Both Stephanie and Amanda said in unison.

The wine was smooth and sweet as it flowed down Amanda's dry throat. Her cheeks flushed with the warmth of the alcohol and she felt relaxed and serene. She texted Brett that they arrived safely, smiled and tucked the phone into her bag. She knew that she needed to relax and give him space and she needed to just be Amanda this weekend and not Brett's mom. She joined the rest of the girls at the table out on the deck and listened to them chatter and the distant waves rumble onto the shore. The salty, sea air was drifting through the screens on the deck and tickling her nose. The beach just had a way of washing away one's worries and soothing a soul. Amanda had missed it. The evening hours passed and the girls wandered off toward their bedrooms to settle in for the night.

Amanda snuggled under the crisp, cotton sheets, a light breeze coming through the open window above her bed. Memories of Todd and the many trips they took to the beach flooded Amanda's still awake mind. She smiled sadly and her heart ached at the thoughts of Todd. She missed him and wished he was here. "I love you!" She whispered into the dark night air. Her eyelids fluttered and sleep overcame her.

The golden light streamed through the shears draped over the windows. Amanda's eyes opened as if they were being tickled by the morning light. She stretched her arms and legs toward the iron bed frame. Her muscles sighed with the stretch and hoped for more. Her feet were slowly drawn to the floor and then scrunched into the soft rug by the bed. Her gaze surveyed the bedroom. It was a pale yellow with white area rugs by the bed, a dresser and rocking chair in the corner. It was modest, yet very cozy. The clock by the bed read 6:38. She thought she was the only person up and decided to grab her running gear out of her bag. She dressed, laced her sneakers and ducked into the bathroom to brush her teeth.

She quietly descended the stairs and added a quick note to the chalk board by the back door.

Went for a run. Be back in 45 minutes. ~ Amanda

The screen door creaked slightly and bounced on the stopper as she walked through toward the beach. The sun warmed her face as she crossed the dunes toward the surf. Amanda felt the morning light perk up her senses and her sadness was lifting, making her heart light. She stretched and decided which way to head on the beach. Amanda started heading north away from the house, moving at a pretty invigorating pace. Her heart was cheering at the feeling of exercise and the sweat was glistening on her skin.

Amanda was in her zone listening to her playlist and looking at the water lapping up on the shore. She saw that there were more runners. She smiled shyly as she thought of the shirtless men running. If Steph were out here with her, she would have nudged her and starting giggling at the sight of a cute man running by. *I'm such girl.* Amanda thought.

Amanda almost returned to her starting point. Forty minutes and five degrees hotter, Amanda was leaning against the railing stretching. The vitamin D was soaking into her pale pores when movement caught Amanda's eye. A man was fighting with his dog to walk along the beach. The dog was preoccupied by a lonely pizza crust that didn't make it into the trash can. She giggled to herself and continued to watch the two of them.

"Hey! Good morning lady! Want coffee?" Stephanie pranced toward her with two sloshing cups in her hand. "Whatcha ya laughin' at this early in the morning?"

"That guy and his dog," Amanda pointed down the beach, giggling, "they're playing an amusing game of tug-o-war over a pizza crust. It just struck me as funny. Thanks" She took the mug. "It smells wonderful!" She brushed a stray hair away from Stephanie's nose. "How'd you sleep?"

"Pretty well, the sound of the waves helped. You?"

Amanda nodded, "That played a part I'm sure. What's on the agenda today?" Amanda sipped her coffee.

"Well, we have a picnic at noon at the house of a movie producer. The company is in talks with him to work on a project and we need to win him over. Tonight he'll decide if he is going to work with us, if he does we will be invited to a beach party to celebrate. You can come to the party, but the picnic is just business so you're free to do whatever you want." There was an anxious look in Steph's eyes and her mind was already focused on work and her pitch.

"You'll do a great job and he'd be crazy not to choose you. I'll hang here at the house and then I'll be ready for your beach party tonight. Do you need me to do anything while you're working?"

"No, just relax. Thanks so much for coming with me! I love you girl!" Stephanie hugged Amanda and kissed her cheek.

"I love you, honey. Go get ready. I'll be up in a minute. I'm getting hungry." Amanda squeezed Steph's hand and turned toward the shoreline with her running shoes airing out on the steps by the dunes. Amanda sat in the sand just above the line of wet sand and began to look for the dog and his walker. They were pretty close to where she was sitting so she was trying not to be too obvious. Her attention returned to her mug and the waves coming up on the sand. All of the sudden she was being knocked on to her back. The mug and swallow of coffee went streaming through the air and came to a rest in the sand with a thud. Amanda shook her head to get a handle on what just happened. There was a furry body trying to lick at her face and sitting on her. She struggled to sit up right.

"Toby! Come here! Bad dog!" The man reached for his collar and yanked Toby off of Amanda. "I'm *so* sorry! You ok?" His green eyes were looking at Amanda with concern.

"Yes! I'm fine." She looked toward the friendly voice and started to laugh. "Come here Toby." She rubbed his ears and he fell over in an attempt to get his belly rubbed too.

"What a gentleman! You sure you're ok? I lost my grip on his leash and he headed right for you. He must've known you were a dog person." The stranger was now sitting in front of Amanda. "This is Toby and I'm Colin. You are?" He held his hand out for her to take.

"Nice to meet you both, I'm Amanda. Please don't worry about this. It will make for a fun story to share later." She took Colin's hand and shook. She was still laughing as her breathing started to slow again and Toby settled in beside her, she took a moment to gaze at Colin. His eyes were green with caramel flecks and his smile was kind and gentle. She could feel her heart skip a beat. He was a handsome man and she was caught off guard by his proximity. She realized that she was still sweaty from her run and probably smelled pretty bad. "Now, I'm sorry. I just finished a run and the bugs are finding me tasty. I should go back to the house, while I still have blood left."

"Of course!" Colin jumped up and offered his hand again. Toby stood but just watched the two humans. Colin slacked on the leash and pulled the mug from the sand. "Here. I hope there wasn't much in there."

"Not even a swallow. Thanks and please don't think I'm rude. I just think it's time for me to go in."

"I understand and Toby and I need to get back to the house for breakfast." Colin turned toward the house down the beach. "How long are going to be here?" He asked while whistling for Toby.

"Just the weekend," Amanda answered.

"Well… I hope to see you again before you leave. I promise I won't tackle you next time I see you." He said smiling with a wink.

"That would be nice… not being tackled… and seeing you" she answered nervously. "Have a great rest of your morning. Enjoy your breakfast!" With that Amanda turned toward the house, grabbed her shoes and walked up the wooden path over the dunes. She could feel the slightest heat in her cheeks and didn't want anyone else to notice.

Colin and Toby turned and headed back to their house. "A funny story of how I met a beautiful lady and how my dog helped me," Colin whispered to himself as he ascended the wooden stairs that took him to his house. His genuine smile warmed him and the mood he was in.

3

Amanda was humming while washing the morning dishes and straightening up the kitchen. She couldn't keep the smile from her mouth. Her run was good this morning. She could get used to running on the beach and hearing the roar of the waves. She could even get used to dogs and strange men knocking her over in the sand. The flush came back to her cheeks and she buzzed around the house picking up wine glasses from last night.

Stephanie came back from her meeting calling through the house for Amanda. "I'm back. Where are you? I'm ready to relax! Amanda….where are you?"

"I'm out here!"

Stephanie came through the screen door carrying a glass of water. "Hey! What've you been up to? Cleaning, I see." She winked and plopped down on the wicker chair beside Amanda. "How was your run this morning? I didn't get a chance to ask you before I left. Everything go ok while we were out?"

"Oh yeah! Sure. Things went fine. You will never believe what happened after you brought me coffee."

"What? You met a cute guy and he swept you off your feet. And now you are leaving me to spend the rest of the weekend him." She cackled.

"No! Not quite." She reached over and playfully punched Stephanie in the shoulder.

Stephanie rubbed her shoulder and pushed out her bottom lip in a pout. She smiled slyly at her friend. "So, what happened?"

"Well, I was on my way back to the house and decided to sit and enjoy the sun and ocean for a few more minutes. I was just soaking up vitamin D, when I was knocked to the sand."

"What? You alright?" Stephanie's worry was plain on her face, scanning Amanda's body.

"Yes, I'm fine. Let me finish my story. I opened my eyes and saw that a big slobbery dog had tackled me." Amanda laughed remembering the funny events from the morning. "So, I regained my balanced and found that this crazy dog belonged to a very apologetic man that was devastated his best friend just knocked me over. He kept saying he was sorry and then asked how long I was in town. He said he hoped to see me again. He wouldn't tackle me if he saw me again."

"Was he cute? What was his name? Where did he come from?" Stephanie would have gone on with her line of questioning but Amanda stopped her by holding up her hand.

"His name is Colin. He lives a couple of houses down. Yes, I guess he is extremely cute." Amanda started to rise and turn toward the house. "What time do we have to be ready for the party?" Amanda quickly changed the subject, hoping Stephanie wouldn't make a big deal about meeting Colin.

Stephanie was gathering her wits as Amanda was quickly throwing questions at her. She knew that Amanda didn't want her to make a big deal of it, but she needed to. "Honey, what did he say? Did he flirt? Do you want to see him again?"

There was the barrage of questions that only Stephanie would think to ask. "Steph, it was nothing. Please don't get your mind all worked up and have some romantic plan forming in that beautiful head of yours. He just apologized for his dog's behavior and then said good bye. There was nothing worth all of your excitement."

"Fine. I want to meet him. I think I should go down to his house and tell him how I feel about his horrible, untrained dog." She said trying to sound angry and disgusted.

"Please don't do that. He felt horrible and I don't want to make him feel worse. It was not a big deal and the dog is a cutie. Please Stephanie, promise me you won't." Amanda felt mortified by the thought of Stephanie going to the man's, Colin, house. "Promise me," a pleading expression passing over her face now.

"Fine… I promise. But if I see him on the beach, I'll give him a piece of my mind." She snapped her head and put her hand on her hips. The ladies walked into the kitchen. The house was buzzing with other conversations but Amanda wanted to go call Brett and read in her room before she needed to get ready for the beach party. Stephanie was being pulled into one of those conversations so Amanda mouthed "Going to call Brett" and continued toward the stairs up to her room.

~φ~

A soft knock on the door startled Amanda from her reading. "Come in."

"Everything good at home?"

"Yes, Brett was napping and getting ready to go out with the guys tonight. He worked this morning and wanted a nap so he wouldn't fall asleep during the movie." Amanda smiled and brushed her hair from her eyes. She placed her book upside down on the night side and crossed her legs on the bed to face Stephanie. "What time do we need to be ready?"

"About an hour, eight o'clock. You ok with coming along?"

"You bet... if you still want me? I don't need to get dressed up, do I? I was just planning on a sun dress. That work?"

"Yes I want you there." She demanded. "I will need a neutral party and my best friend to hold my hand. Sun dress will be perfect." Stephanie was turning toward the door and remembered, "We're walking to the party, just so you know." With a smile, she turned and headed toward her room next door. She left the door open just enough that the chatter from the TV downstairs whiffed in the room. "See you in a bit." Stephanie sang as she entered her door. Amanda walked toward the window and could see Toby running along the shore line. Colin was throwing a tennis ball up and down the beach. A grin crept across her face. She missed having a dog and loved watching him frolic in the surf. Colin was fun to watch too. He was muscular. His hair was coppery with nature's highlights and his eyes were happy and bright. In the few minutes that Amanda had met him, she felt like she had a good idea of the kind of man he was. She felt funny thinking about a man this way. Another man was not something that she thought about much. Todd was her best friend and the love of her life, but now that he was gone, she worried that spending her years alone would be lonely and a sad reminder that her best friend was gone. Maybe Colin could be a distraction? Amanda giggled like a school girl. Warmth colored her cheeks lightly as she pulled a light rose sundress from her closet; it matched the color of her cheeks.

As Amanda finished readying herself, she made sure that she looked pretty and natural. She didn't want to look done up like some of the other girls that would probably be at the party. She took a glance in the mirror, one last time and walked out into the hall, just as Stephanie had exited her room.

Stephanie's eyes lit up and she smiled at the site of Amanda walking toward her. "Wow, lady! You look amazing!"

"Thanks! You look hot!" The women walked closer to each other, linked hands and walked down the stairs together. "Let's do this!"

Stephanie squeezed her hand and they walked out the back door toward the beach. The glowing moon was rising through the wispy clouds of sunset. The waves were lapping on the sand and the houses' lights twinkled like Christmas time. They headed about four houses up the beach where music was dancing through the air. The laughter and voices were coming from the pool, so they climbed the dunes and could see the shimmery, golden light from the torches flaming along the deck.

"Ok, we're here. Come with me and meet the head honcho." Stephanie pulled Amanda toward her co-workers and wrapped her arm around her waist when they got to the circle of business taking place. "This is my dearest friend, Amanda. She is a teacher from Pennsylvania." Stephanie declared as she stood front and center of a silver headed man dress like a Ralph Lauren model. The conversation continued about Stephanie and Amanda's growing up together. Stephanie couldn't stand the small talk any farther. "Are we getting the job or not, Mr. Brodbeck? I am tired of the niceties. Get it over with? Are we making a movie?" Stephanie's passion and confidence were spilling out of her and she was breathless.

Mr. Brodbeck chuckled and scanned Stephanie and her colleagues. "Of course, we have a deal. I love all of the ideas and I'm very excited to start working." Stephanie released Amanda's hand and pulled her into a hug and then went into work mode. The talking began to revolve around books and actors and things that didn't relate to Amanda's world.

As they planned and brainstormed, Amanda wondered down toward the beach. There was a small fire area with chairs and benches. There was no one else there, so it was quiet and Zen. Amanda pulled her legs under her as she cocooned into the chair closest to the fire. She closed her eyes just remembering a time when Todd and Brett had roasted marshmallows and laughed at the sugar torches they made. Her face warmed with a smile and glowed from the fire.

4

"Would you mind some company? I don't want to bother you."

Amanda heard a familiar voice but couldn't place it. She opened her eyes and looked into fire dancing in a set of green eyes.

"No, please sit down." she gestured to the empty chair beside her.

"What were you thinking about sitting all alone?"

"One time my son and husband roasted marshmallows. Well, not really roasting them as much as lighting them on fire like torches. They were laughing so hard and acting like they were twirling batons." She giggled a little and looked away from those attentive eyes.

"Where are your son and husband tonight?"

"My son is at home working his summer job and my husband passed away two years ago."

"Oh… I …am… so sorry!"

She waved his apology away, "How could you have known. We had a great life together and he gave me a wonderful boy." Amanda smiled and rubbed her arms with her hands to warm her skin. She then glanced over at the warm, concerned eyes gazing at her. "Really, it's ok." She reassured him.

He looked at her shyly and tried to think if something to say to make him not feel like such a jerk. "Here take this." He slid his arms and head out of the sweatshirt he was wearing to reveal a thermal shirt. "I know it doesn't go with your dress but it will keep the chill away." She nodded and whispered thanks. "I didn't think I'd see you again, after this morning's bizarre introduction. Again, sorry about Toby. Did you have a good rest of your day? No one else attacked you, I hope?"

Amanda let out a nervous laugh. "Nope, no one attacked me. It was a good day. I hung out by the house while the rest of the gang was meeting with Mr. Brodbeck. What about you?" She felt very at ease talking to this stranger. He seemed comfortable with himself and didn't put off airs like some of the other people that were at this party.

"Well, I did some work, took a nap with Toby and cleaned up to come here."

"What are doing here tonight? Work or pleasure?"

Colin chuckled. "Well, that depends on how you look at it." He said with a wink. "I work with Mr. Brodbeck, which is work. I enjoy talking to you, which is pleasure."

"I see, work and pleasure." Amanda was blushing. *Wow, he was smooth.* Why are you sitting with me? I am certainly not the prettiest woman here or the youngest."

"Why not you? You're gorgeous and honest, which is foreign in today's world. I've met many women that will tell me anything they think I want to hear and stroke my ego. You treat me as if we've been friends and you give it to me straight with no bull." Colin began to think this woman was fantastic. She made him feel fresh and willing to be himself.

Amanda nodded as he spoke and panic slapped her in the face. *What do I say to that?* "So who are you that these women are quick to please you?" *Keep breathing.* She was now thinking and hoping he wouldn't be offended by her cheekiness.

Colin chuckled and pulled his legs to his chest as he sat in an empty chair beside her. *How much do I tell her?* "Well, I am a writer, director, musician and a famous, hot actor. Maybe you have seen some of my work?"

"Now you're playing. Tell me your favorite project. I do have some knowledge of current entertainment."

"Just a writer," Colin smiled and thought a moment. "No one has ever asked me about my favorite project. That's a tough one. I think it would be The Lemonade Project. It was a great story with great people but it raised awareness for children's cancer and research. I can't watch it without crying."

"You did not do that? I love that story. My students wrote letters to the kids in the hospital and raised money for them. I even had a few kids that went to see the patients at Christmas. I wanted to make them aware there are other people in the world that don't have what they have. I can't believe that was you?"

Her dark eyes softened and looked at Colin with appreciation. "Thank you. It was a great project."

His shoulders slouched on himself and he looked out toward to the sea shyly. "I was not expecting that reaction. I didn't think you would know it."

"You're welcome." Sitting up a bit straighter, he turned toward Amanda and tilted his head in interest. "What do you teach?"

"Third grade. My students this year were very compassionate. They loved talking about the friends they were making all over the country from the letters and projects we did. Some of them Skype their new friends."

Colin listened. She was beautiful and wow, what an important lesson to teach to your students. "That sounds fantastic. They probably loved coming to your class. I needed more teachers like you when I was in grade school. Where do you teach?"

"Outside of Philly. Money is not much of an issue for most of the families. That's why I wanted them to get out of their safe zone and meet kids that are different from them. Does that sound crazy?"

"Not at all. I think in today's world too many people only think about themselves so it's a good lesson to give them. More like... not crazy, wise and enriching."

She rubbed her arms that were warmly inside his sweatshirt. They both sat quietly for a minute and watched the moonlight dance on the waves. He stood and placed a small log on the fire and the flames flickered and snapped. He glanced at her as he sat back down and she quietly smiled at him. The quiet was nice but he wanted to talk to her more. *What else could I ask her?*

She yawned and covered her mouth with embarrassment. "So sorry. It is past my bedtime. I should go back." She rose from the chair and yawned again.

"Wait! I'll walk you. You never know who or what could jump on you out there alone." He jumped out of his chair as she started walking toward the house. A goofy look crossed his face as he remembered this morning.

"Oh, ok. That would be nice. I definitely don't need to be knocked over or licked again." She giggled. "I'll go tell Stephanie." As she turned, her dress flared out and Colin saw just enough of her upper thigh to make him have some dirty thoughts. He shook his head to try to behave.

Amanda whispered her plan to Steph and headed in the direction of the fire. She saw Colin leaning against the railing. He was very handsome and the small fire behind him was turning his form into a glowing ember. She crept, so she could enjoy watching him. Two steps away, his head turned slightly and that shy smile crossed his face. He held out his hand and she took it. He tucked it warmly in to the crook of his elbow. Their shoulders brushed against each other as they walked. The sparks from the fire were now between the two of them.

They walked and talked more about his work and her teaching. They arrived at the house and sat by the dunes. The conversation took on the rhythm of the waves coming in and going out. Neither was apprehensive about sharing things. They were open books. Colin shared that he had two sons and a daughter. Amanda explained about Todd's death and how Brett was the only man in her life. They laughed at stories about their families and sat comfortably in the moon light.

The conversation lulled and they both yawned in unison. A laugh escaped as they both stood. "I guess I should let you go."

"I need my rest so I can be nurse in the morning. I also want to run again in the morning. I guess you're right." She reached over and lightly touched his arm. "Thank you for keeping me company and walking me home. It was great." She smiled and squeezed his arm before she let go.

"My pleasure." He reached for her hand and kissed her knuckles. She smiled and turned toward the house.

"Good night, Colin. Thanks again." She turned and was walking backwards up the plank walk. He waved and turned toward his house. "Oh! Colin, wait!" She ran back toward him. He must've walked toward her to close the gap and she misjudged, running right into him. He caught her before she fell into the sand again. "Your sweatshirt." She panted.

"You keep it. I'll see you another time if you keep it." He looked like he was concocting a plot to see her again but didn't say anything.

He was still holding her elbows. "Stay warm and good night again." He leaned down and gave her a light, sweet kiss on her check.

She held her breath and tried to keep her heart in her chest. Butterflies were fluttering in her belly and she wanted to kiss him back but resisted. She looked into his eyes and they were warm and dark. The moon was making them shimmer. She blushed and backed away from him. "Good night!" *I'm such a chicken.* As she walked to the house, she glanced back. Colin was still standing at the end of the plank walk. She waved.

Amanda reached the porch and opened the screen door. Colin was running up the walk. "What... are... you doing? You don't live here." She was laughing at him as he huffed and puffed from the jog.

He was panting and resting on his hands on his thighs while he caught his breath. He held up a finger and looked at her. "Would you... like to... have ...lun...ch? Tom...orrow? I could pick you up around 12." The porch light was making a halo around her head. "I'd understand if you think it's too much of me in a 24 hour period but I was enjoying our talking and don't want it to be over quite yet."

She grinned again and sighed. She was giving in to him and herself. "That would be nice. See you then." She went to turn the door knob and she felt his breath on the back of her neck and the fluttering came. *Do I turn around?* "Good night, again" She said without turning around.

He cupped her elbow and gave her a slight tug to spin her toward him for a light kiss on her cheek. When she didn't pull away, he slowly moved his face to meet her eyes, but they were turned to the ground. He took his free hand and gently tilted her chin up and her eyes met his. He could see fear and desire. He tried to convey 'its ok.' with his look. She exhaled and leaned into him. He placed his lips on her mouth and felt a little of that fear melt away. She reached for his shoulders then slid her hands around his neck. This was not going to be one of the passionate, lost in the moment, fingers tangling in your hair kinds of kisses, but was gentle and allowed their bodies to become attuned to each other.

"Amanda? Is that you? I thought you would be in bed sound asleep by now."

Amanda looked at Stephanie trying not to let the embarrassment show too much. "Colin walked me home and we were talking. We lost track of time and now he was making sure that I got in ok." *Smooth, real smooth, Amanda.* Colin chuckled and turned to face Stephanie's piercing eyes.

"Hi! I'm Colin." He smiled offering his hand to Stephanie and then turned back to Amanda, "Thank you for a lovely time tonight, Amanda. I'll see you tomorrow. Sleep well." He turned and walked back toward the beach and his house.

"Colin, dear, please come this way. It's closer." Stephanie was smiling, trying not to laugh as he sheepishly walked back and followed the two ladies through the house to the front door. He made it to the door with Stephanie saying good night and Amanda hiding behind her. The front door closed and he finally let out the breath he didn't know he was holding.

The girls stood inside the door and laughed. "You'd better get to your room young lady. I can't believe you were kissing a boy on the porch tonight. Get yourself ready for bed!" Stephanie called to Amanda has she chased her up the stairs. They were both laughing and tripping as they ascended the stairs.

Colin began to laugh too. The front windows were open. He could hear the whole thing. "Good night Amanda. Good luck!" He whispered as he left the front porch.

5

Sunlight peeked through the wooden slates of the blinds. A growl and stretch came from under the sheet. Two brown eyes peered over the edge of the bed and a dripping tongue was waiting for a moving game of chase. The steady beat of Toby's tail was making music on the wood floor. Eye contact was made and Toby made a move toward a greeting kiss. "I'm up! I'm up! Move your furry butt and I'll get some clothes on." Colin rubbed the top of his head and walked to the bathroom. Toby trotted after him. "Buddy, I can handle this myself. Thanks," as he closed the door.

Two excruciatingly long minutes later, Toby pranced as his man opened the door. "Let's go you impatient creature. Toby, if you see that pretty lady today, please don't tackle her. I want her to like us both and not run the other way when she sees us coming." Colin clipped the leash to Toby's collar and unlocked the back door. As soon as his paws hit the porch, Toby took off for the sand. Colin looked like he was being swept off his feet and out the door. "Take it easy buddy. Pace yourself." Colin smiled and thought he should say the same thing to himself. Maybe he should not have kissed her twice last night. *What was I thinking?* He was watching Toby play tag with the waves, when he heard a voice behind him.

"Good morning." There was a hint of laughter in her words and she was trying not to run over and knock him over for a bit of pay back. Colin turned, but before he could say anything, Toby caught sight of her and yanked the leash in her direction. She was wearing black running pants, a pink tank and baseball cap. Her chocolate brown eyes were twinkling with the morning sun and her skin was glistening with sweat. Toby charged toward her and sat right by her feet. "What did you do to him?" She said surprised by his patience in getting to her.

"We had a long talk yesterday. I explained that women will not stick around if we can't greet them appropriately. We worked on it all afternoon. I guess it paid off." Colin was facing her now and was just a few feet from her. Tucking his free hand in his pocket, he tried to think of something great to say. "Have a good run?" he blurted out.

"Yes, thank you. I was headed in when I saw Toby bounding down the beach, thought I would see hi."

"Not going to stay and play with Toby? He's grown quite smitten with you." Colin looked down and Toby was now wrapped around her legs, rubbing his head all over her pants. He chuckled aloud. "Toby, she doesn't want fur pants." He snapped the leash and Toby lifted his eyes with an annoyed look, then continued to rub her. Amanda was scratching his head between his ears. He was purring like a kitten.

"I have a lunch date I need to get ready for and three babies back at the house to tend to. It's always a pleasure, Toby, but I don't want my date to think I have bad hygiene habits." She winked at Toby and stood up straight. "You two go have a great walk and I will go tend to my patients." She smiled warmly at Colin and began to walk toward the house.

"Lucky guy to be having lunch with you. Have a good time." He joked and winked at Amanda. "See you."

"Yes you will!" She waved, turned and jogged up the walk. His eyes were still on her and she wanted to turn and look at him but she was blushing so bright, she was afraid that he would see if from there. Amanda focused on not tripping over the wooden planks and safely made it to the house. She turned around now, knowing he couldn't see her. He was being dragged down the beach.

~(♪~

"*Amanda*! I need water and crackers." A demanding voice called from upstairs.

"Coming, Boss!" Amanda carried a small tray of crackers, two bottles of water and two Tylenol.

"Thank you! I'm so glad you're here to take care of me. What would I do without you?"

"Drag your lazy butt out of bed or suffer dehydration in your bed." Amanda placed the tray on the night stand and walked toward the door. "I'm getting a shower. You need anything else Your Highness?"

"Why do you have to be like that? I'm in pain." Stephanie was smiling with puppy dog eyes.

"Oh, please! You knew what you were doing. Besides I have a date and I don't want to take care of your lazy butt. Get up and take care of yourself." She put her hands on her hips and huffed out the door.

"Hey, you better fill me in on all the details when you get back. I want to hear all about it. I live vicariously through your romantic interludes." still giving puppy eyes.

"You're pathetic and you know I'll share. I gave details last night, you just can't remember." Amanda turned and the expression on her face changed. Her brows were squeezed together and her eyes were sad. "Steph, be honest. It's ok that I like him and I want to see him again?"

"Aw, honey. Yes it's completely ok. Todd would love to see you happy and making the best of your life. You know you would've wanted the same for him if the roles were reversed. Right?"

"You're right. It has been so long since I have been attracted to someone that wasn't my husband. I felt like I cheated on him last night and all I did was kiss him."

"Sweetheart, come here." Stephanie wrapped her arms around Amanda and kissed her cheek. "You go and have a great lunch. No worries. Enjoy his company." She pushed her away and slapped her butt. "Now get your stinky ass in the shower or he'll never want to see you again."

Both girls laughed and Amanda headed to her room. Amanda hugged herself and thought about what Steph said. She was absolutely right. Todd would want her to be happy, whether that was alone or with someone. A sad smile crossed her face as she stepped in the shower.

6

The breeze was warmly blowing by the front porch. Colin was downing the last swallow of his water. He was looking over the dunes to the house next door. He smiled and squeezed the bottle in his nervous hands. He was excited to see Amanda but he was worried he was moving too fast for both of them. He should have never kissed her last night. They just met and it was too much. She lost her husband two years ago. He divorced about 3 years ago, which was a bit different. He wasn't happy with his wife, but she didn't die. Losing a spouse when you aren't ready is just so… He shook his head and looked at the clock. "Two minutes 'til twelve, crap! I have to go!" Colin grabbed his keys, wallet, and phone and patted Toby's head. "Take a nap buddy! I'll see you in a bit." Toby walked in three circles and plopped down on the sunny spot on the rug. With that, Colin turned the knob and walked out the door. The lock clicked and Toby sighed.

He sprinted up the walk and leaned on the railing to the steps to catch his breath. "You're late!" a stern voice growled from the front door. He looked up to see Stephanie behind the screen door. She smiled and walked out. "Take good care of my Amanda, ok? She is an amazing person but she's still a bit unsure. Use your head and your heart to treat her right. Got me?" Her voice sounded like something between an angry parent and a loving sister. Colin nodded and walked up the stairs. He put out his hand for Stephanie to shake.

"I completely get you. I'll do what you say. I'll tread lightly because quite honestly I'm afraid what you'd do to me."

"I'd be too if I were you." A light, happier voice said through the screen. "Stephanie, you play nice with my new friend."

"I am," Stephanie relaxed and released a breath. "You kids have fun! Where are you going for lunch?" Looking at Colin.

"Seafood Shack... that work?" His voice sounded a bit unsure and nervous. He was looking at both Stephanie and Amanda as they both stood on the porch looking at him. He tilted his hand to the side and his eyes were catching the sunlight like emeralds.

"Sounds great! Let's go before Steph invites herself along." Amanda took a deep breath, flitted down the stairs and grabbed Colin's arm. She looked into his surprised but pleased eyes and pulled him down the walk. "Are we driving?" She asked as they reached the driveway.

"We probably should. We can walk around town after lunch if you want." He raised an eyebrow asking if she was ok with that option.

"Sounds good! Take me to the car then, sir."

Colin was intrigued by this woman. She seemed more relaxed and sure of herself than she did yesterday. Maybe she was nervous and it came off this way. "Your chariot, my lady." He opened the door for her. He was saying a quiet thank you to himself. The car was clean and neat. It even smelled good. He loved his car. He bought it after he wrote and made one of his first big movies. He always wanted a Range Rover, now it was a bit out of date but it was his favorite car and he loved it.

He walked over to the driver's side and arranged himself in his seat. The engine purred to life and they were headed to lunch. The first few minutes were full of the humming of the radio. Then Amanda broke the silence. "Sorry about Stephanie. She tends to get a bit over protective."

"She must care for you very much. How long have you two been friends?"

Amanda watched his face. He was calm and didn't cringe at the mention of Stephanie. "We have been friends since first grade. We grew up together and have been there for each other through all life's events. She can be intense."

"Why are you laughing? She's one scary lady."

"Sorry. I remember when she meet Todd for the first time and found out he was taking me out on a date. He wouldn't hold my hand and it took him two weeks to call me again. I love her and I know that she means well." The Range Rover slowed and turned into a parking lot. The Seafood Shack was right on the beach. The paint on the old clapboards was peeling but the deck was giving off a fun loving vibe. The sounds of food being prepared came from the screen door by the kitchen and laughter and conversations made it feel warm and welcoming. "It smells yummy and the view is beautiful." They rounded the corner and saw the hostess standing, waiting for them. The water was blue green and lapping on to the beach. Fluffy white clouds were blowing across the sky with a light warm breeze.

"It's a local hidden treasure," he said smiling gently at her. "Two for the deck if you could please, Beth." Colin turned back to Amanda. "She is one of my daughter's friends."

Amanda made a silent "Oh" and nodded at him.

"Right this way Mr. Marks." Beth said warmly and led them to a table on the deck. "Riley will be your server this afternoon. Enjoy your meal." She laid the menus in front of both of them and walked back toward the hostess station. "Oh, Mr. Marks, when will Tiffani be coming up? I can't wait to see her." She was bouncing on her toes in excitement.

"I believe she will be up next week with her mom and brothers."

"Great! Thanks! See you later!" Beth skipped back to the station to seat the next party.

"So how old are your kids?"

"Tiffani is my youngest at 16, Patrick is 18 and David is almost 20. Both Patrick and David are in college. Tiffani goes to a private school on Long Island, called St. Dominic. The boys went there too. There mom grew up on Long Island so she wanted them to go to school there. I lived on Long Island but after the divorce moved to Manhattan." He looked shyly down at his menu and back at Amanda through his eye lashes.

"Colin," Amanda reached over and took his hand. "We both have a past. Without our pasts shaping who we are and taking us through life, we wouldn't be here together now. I don't expect you to not talk about your ex-wife and I know I will talk about my husband." She paused and pushed her windblown hair behind her ear and bit down on her lip before continuing. "Now, if you start talking about a current girlfriend or wild times you had with other women, I will have to leave you seating alone. Got it?" She smiled playfully, winking at him. She gently squeezed his hand before she put it back on the menu.

"Yes, ma'am. Got it." He released the breath he was holding and seriously looked at his menu to try to pick something.

The meal went smoothly and conversation flowed easily. They both relaxed and enjoyed the atmosphere and the company. Amanda was talking about Brett. Colin was watching how her face lit up when she mentioned her son. Colin began to think about how the sun brought out the red and blonde in her brown hair. Her milk chocolate eyes made him freeze when she looked into his eyes.

Amanda was turning the conversation to him. She wanted to know about his job and his family. She listened with attentive ears. His hair was a mess, which was the style. He dressed well, but not like model from J. Crew. He presented himself in a way that made him look like he was himself without any airs. He spoke with a relaxed, strong voice. His eyes stayed on Amanda's, which was hard for her sometimes. She would nervously look at her napkin or the other people in the restaurant.

Their plates had been cleared and the bill paid. Colin leaned toward Amanda. "Are you ready for that walk through town?"

"Yes." She placed her napkin on the table. She pushed her chair back to stand up and Colin was offering his hand. She smiled and lightly slid hers into his. "Thank you."

They walked out of the restaurant and looked in the windows of the shops that lined the street. Amanda noticed how some of the passersby were looking at him and her. *What were they staring at? Were they wondering why he was with me?*

"What are you thinking about? You have a look and you left me."

"Oh, nothing. What were you saying, sorry?" Her eyes looked apologetic.

"You are a horrible liar. Spill it!" He squeezed her hand gently joking.

"Everyone that walks past us is staring. Why? Do I have something on me?" She stopped and turned to him.

"Well… I am guessing here… but I would say they are trying to figure out who we are. They expect to see celebrities and are trying to figure out if we are. I have been coming here most of my life and the tourists will do that." He looked into her eyes and shrugged his shoulders.

"I see. So it's not that you're with me and not some super model?" She playfully bumped into his shoulder.

"Super models are overrated and not nearly as much fun as you." He bumped her back. They began walking again. He could feel Amanda relax a little and she begin to look around and take in the sights.

They had walked and ended up back at the Rover. "Would you like to go back and spend some time with Stephanie?" Colin said with a slight sadness in his voice. He knew she was leaving tomorrow.

"She may be working. Let me see what she's doing." Amanda pulled out her phone and texted Steph.

Hey, lady

Hows the date

Great you working

yes

Mind if I hang with Colin a little longer

Nope dinner tonight

OK

bring wine and colin

will do love you

love you 2

"What are you smiling about?" Colin glanced over at her phone with curiosity.

"Stephanie invited you to dinner if you don't have any plans. She is working so I am all yours… if you want to stay a little longer?" Amanda asked with a questioning raise of her eye brow.

Colin sighed. "If you don't mind my company, I'd love to keep you for a while longer. We could go take Toby down to the beach. Maybe you can make him a well behaved dog?" *Thank you, she wants to stay with me and have dinner too. I hope she isn't doing it just to be polite. I really like being with her. I don't have to pretend to be someone I'm not. I get to relax and be me. I hope she likes what she sees so far.*

"Hey! Where did you go? You had this sad look in your eyes." She held her breath hoping that he would say no.

"I was thinking that I enjoy being myself with you and I hope that you like… never mind. I should have stopped and said nothing." He ran a hand through his hair. Amanda could see a lonely, insecure man hiding inside this confident exterior.

Amanda smiled and put her hand over his. "I'm glad. I feel the same way. I like spending time with you and I'm glad that we can spend some time together."

He pulled her hand to his mouth and placed a light kiss on the top of her hand. "Thank you." He whispered.

~ℓ~

Toby greeted them with a prance and lots of kisses. Amanda looked around the house. There were pictures of his kids and parents. They all looked happy and loving. Colin went to the kitchen and returned with two bottles of water. He slipped his shoes off and placed them behind the front door. He reached to the screen door and locked it. Amanda slipped off her shoes and placed them beside his. She stood up and saw him smiling at her. "What?" She was blushing slightly, but was trying to remain calm with him so close to her. He was close enough that she could feel his breath on her ear and smell his fabric softener.

"Water?" He handed her a bottle and was smiling, enjoying the reaction he got from her. *She must feel the same way about me.* He was reassuring himself. "Come here Toby. Let's go for a w-a-l-k." Toby sat while Colin hooked his leash, and then started to dance wildly. "Ok, Amanda. You ready for this adventure?" He was shyly smiling at her, hoping she would pick up on the double meaning in what he just said.

"As ready as I'll ever be," she replied nervously. "You'll stay with me and not leave me... alone with Toby, right? I don't think I could handle him without you."

"You can handle... Toby. You're stronger than you think." He winked at her and offered his hand. She let out a smile and laced his fingers with hers.

7

*A*manda returned home from walking Toby on the beach to get ready for dinner. While she was in her room freshening up, she heard footsteps in the hall. Probably Steph coming to her room to get something, she caught sight of a figure out of the corner eye leaning against her door way. She jumped, startled. He was tall, handsome and giving her a sexy smile. Before she found her voice, he walked toward her and spoke. "You left these at my house," placing her shoes at the end of the bed. He continued toward her sitting at the desk. She was facing the doorway now. He knelt down. He was inches from her face, he whispered, "I need to do something that I have been thinking about all day, but if you don't want me to, tell me now." He hesitated to hear a response... nothing. He placed his lips gently on hers and kissed her with tenderness, passion and desire. She kissed him back and hooked her hands to the back of his neck. Both of their bodies relaxed into each other.

They broke apart and were looking into each other's eyes. Amanda rubbed her thumbs on his cheeks and smiled. "Thank you. I'm glad you did that."

He took his hands from her waist, pulled her to stand in front of him and hugged her. "It was killing me. I wanted to do that since I picked you up at noon." He was talking into her hair and then stepped back to reveal a warm grin and loving green eyes.

She playfully pulled him by the hand to the stairs. "Ok, maybe one more..." She turned right before she descended the first step. She kissed him lightly on the cheek, and then paused right in front of his lips. She could hear his breathing hitch and his body leaned toward her. He stepped on the first step, so they were the looking directly into each other's eyes. "...or I can make you wait until after dinner." She flirted.

Colin pulled her hips toward him and planted his mouth on hers. It was more playful that the last. He wanted her to know that he wanted her and was willing to play too. He pushed her away and gave that sexy smile again. "I can play dirty too, missy!" He walked down the steps without looking back at her. She was standing at the top catching her breath. "Are you coming to dinner?" He offered his hand from the bottom of the stairs and she ran down to meet him.

Everyone was seated around the dining room table. Glasses of wine, platters of spaghetti, baskets of garlic bread sat at each end of the table. Laughing, storytelling and a light sea breeze blew through the open windows. Stephanie was watching Amanda and Colin from the opposite side of the table. They were talking with others at the table, telling stories and laughing. She noticed that he would reach over and hold her hand while they listened to stories. Stephanie was happy to see the two of them together and enjoying one another but also worried that Colin's intentions were not as true as Amanda's. She didn't want her best friend to get hurt.

Stephanie rose from the table and began to carry dishes to the kitchen. Colin rose and followed with a handful of platters. "Hey! Are you ok? You have been quiet all evening." Colin said to the back of Steph as she loaded the dishwasher.

"Sure, just enjoying my last night at the beach with my best friend. I'm glad to see that you and Amanda are enjoying each other. Did you guys have a good afternoon?" She busied herself with the dishes and tried to keep her calm."

"Yeah, we did have a good day. We walked around town and on the beach. She's a warm, caring, open and honest woman. She makes me want to be myself all the time and not to be afraid of it." He said running his hand through his hair nervously. "Stephanie, I don't want to hurt your friend. Please know that." His eyes were pleading with her as she turned from the sink to look at him.

A tear ran down Steph's face, "Oh, I'm so glad to hear you say that. I have seen her struggle with losing Todd and then being unsure about seeing you. She is strong but fragile at the same time. Please be good to her. Or so help me!" She raised her fist at him and gave him the sternest look she had. "Got it!?!?"

"What are you two discussing now?" Amanda said as she crossed the kitchen carrying empty glasses. "Steph, you aren't still reading Colin the riot act, I hope." She began the rinsing the glasses and placing them on the top shelf of the open dishwasher.

"No, honey. I was just..."

Colin interrupted, "You're friend wanted to make sure my intentions were honorable." He looked at Steph and winked. He completely understood why she was so overprotective, but he wanted her to trust him and believe him. "I'll go get more stuff off the table."

Amanda was smiling next to Stephanie, "you ok? You look like you've been crying."

"I'm fine. Just sad our weekend is coming to a close." She reached over and rubbed Amanda's shoulder. "Can we do this again this summer? Maybe with the kids? What do you think?"

"I would love that. I am sure Brett would love to come up here too." Amanda continued cleaning up the kitchen. Colin returned with more stuff off the table. "Is the table cleared?"

"Just needs wiped down," he grabbed the clean cloth off the counter and walked back to the dining room.

"He's a keeper. He cleans. Does he cook?" Stephanie joked as she finally came out of her worried state.

"He does cook but not that well, Toby is the only one that enjoys it." Colin answered as he entered the kitchen with a cloth in his hand.

"Now that you kids have helped clear the table, why don't you go outside and enjoy the cool breeze and the moon light." Stephanie backed up against the sink and shooed the both out of them out of the kitchen.

~✺~

Colin and Amanda were sitting on a wicker sofa within the screen porch. A great day was winding down and the weekend was almost over. Colin slowly slid his arm over her shoulders and felt her slide closer and nuzzle into his side. A smile spread over his face and he breathed in her warm and light coconut scent. His heart beat pounded and he was trying to slow his breathing. Amanda slid her right arm across his torso and tickled his side. "What are you thinking about?"

"Hey! No tickling" He took her hand and laced his fingers through hers. "When are you leaving tomorrow?"

"I think we are driving into the city around 10:00 and then I have to catch the 1:00 train home. Are you leaving or staying?" She said resting her chin on his chest, looking through her eye lashes.

"Well, I was going back to city but since you are leaving, maybe I will stay here and get some peace and quiet." He replied jabbing her in the side.

"Really?"

"NO! I have to head back to the city but I have to wait for the cleaning crew, they don't get here until 12. Maybe I will see you before you catch your train? What station are you leaving from?"

"Penn." Amanda turned her head and looked out to the sea.

"Would you like to see me again?" His voice sounded low and unsure.

"Of course, I want to see you again." She snuggled in closer to his side and looked up at him. "You are great. You have brightened my life and I am so glad that we got to spend this weekend together. I hope that we can have more time."

He pulled her face up to his and kissed her. He wanted her to feel all the hope and desire he had brewing within him. The time they had together was short but his heart was beating faster and his breathing was all over the place. His hands were sweating and he had trouble thinking straight. As he pulled away for a moment of clarity, "I guess that is a yes, to seeing me again." He smiled sheepishly. "Can we exchange numbers?"

Amanda smiled and touched his cheek. "Being with you makes me feel young, happy and … like a teenager on summer vacation." She snuggled back down into the crook of Colin's neck and closed her eyes listening to the waves on the shore. "I'll give you my number."

"Thank you for being you." He squeezed her and winked when she looked at him. "Are you cold?" He pulled the afghan from the back of the sofa and draped it over both of them. They both sighed into each other and drifted off to sleep listening to hearts beating, waves rolling and wind chimes tinkling.

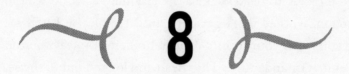

8

The morning sun was giving an orange and pink tint to everything. Amanda and Colin stretched out on the couch. Amanda snuggled into his chest and he drew her closer. "Good morning," they whispered to each other. Amanda looked up slowly to see his sleepy green eyes gazing back at her. The corners of his eyes turned up with his smile. Both of his strong arms pulled her up. They were nose to nose. Their hearts were beating quickly in beat with each other.

Colin's chest was rising with his quickening breath. He leaned in a bit and kissed her fore head. "Good morning. Did you sleep well? I didn't mean to spend the night, but I can't think of a better place to wake up." His eyes dropped shyly and pulled her even closer.

"Yes, I did. Thank you." Amanda started to pull away to a sitting up position. She stretched her arms over her head. "You have very handsome bed head." She ruffled his hair and brushed her hand lightly down his rough, unshaven cheek.

Colin blushed and ran a hand through his disheveled hair. "No need to tease. You've got bed head too, you know," tugging on a strand of hair. He turned to stand up and wake his stiff muscles. He reached his long arms over his head and mumbled, "Although, it's beautiful!"

"What was that?" Amanda curiously looked at him as she folded the afghan and flung it over the couch."Couldn't hear you." she held her hand to her ear.

Amanda was spun around and in his arms in a split second. He wrapped his arms around her and looked into alert brown eyes. "I said you're beautiful!" He leaned down and greeted her good morning. His body coming alive being so close to her.

"Oh!" She said pressed against his lips. Amanda's fingers tangled in his bed tossed hair. Her mind was racing. *This was bad and really good. What am I going to do? This man is wonderful. I'm so scared, but I love kissing him.* She pushed her thoughts out of her mind and lost herself his warm embrace and loving kiss. A moan escaped her lips and she allowed her body to warm and awaken to his closeness.

Colin felt her body mold against him and her kiss morphed into raw passion and emotion. He hoped that she could feel the same from him. Today she was going home. *When will I see her again? I am falling in love with this beautiful woman. How am I going to do this? How am I going to say good-bye? It was so soon.*

The kissing was interrupted by a clearing throat. "Come up for air. You know we have to pack and get back to the city." Stephanie was watching smugly from the kitchen door.

Amanda and Colin looked at each other and replied to Stephanie in unison, "Sorry." They joined hands and pushed past her to enter the kitchen. They stole two mugs of coffee off the counter as Amanda led Colin up to her room. "I'll be ready when it is time to go." Amanda called down the stairs before she closed the door. She walked to the closet, pulled out the suitcase and threw it on the bed. "Would you like to help me pack?"

"As much as I would love to fondle your intimates," he said picking up a lacey pair of panties. "I should go home and get myself ready to get back to the city. Toby is probably ready to go out." As he said these words to Amanda, her face changed and his heart tightened. Her eyes began to turn sad and he recognized a longing look that reflected his own. "Not that I don't want to stay but it's going to be hard enough to say good bye to you later. At least we're alone at the moment to say good-bye." He gave an apologetic look and grabbed her hand. He pulled her onto his lap and caressed her back and traced the tip of his nose up her neck to her ear. "Please give me just a moment to bid you good-bye." He put his hands on each side of her face and kissed her. The fear of the unknown and longing was heating up making it hard for both to say good-bye.

She wanted this man but was afraid it was happening too fast, too soon. This man was so warm, caring, and honest. He wasn't Todd, but he was lovely. She hoped that she would find answers and he would be in them. She needed to talk to him before her courage faltered.

"Colin, please let me say this." she pulled away and avoided his eyes. I have enjoyed our time together but what's going to happen now? I have no right to ask you to be mine, no matter how juvenile that sounds. I want to say thank you and I hope that we can remember this time fondly. I don't want to push myself on you or have any expectations, so we can part ways today and have no pressure."

"Wait a minute!" hurt in his voice. "You don't want to stay in touch or make plans. Am I hearing you correctly?" His face was twisted and confused. "You don't want to see me again?" He said backing away.

"NO! I want to see you again but…" she reached out to comfort him.

"But what? I've loved being with you. I don't want to say good-bye. I want to make plans and see you again. I don't want to throw away this great time we've had or the good times that we could have. Are you saying these things because you think I'm the kind of guy that only wants a fling?" his pain and sincerity was lacing his words. "I want to 'belong' to someone and I want them to want the same." His eyes were pleading.

"You lead a different life than I do. I assumed that you didn't want any attachments. I just figured..." Amanda reached for his hand to apologize for her misunderstanding.

Colin took her hand and pulled her into his arms. "I'm not sure where this is going ... I want you. Please say you'll try." He brushed his thumb across her cheek lightly.

She leaned her cheek into his touch and closed her eyes. "I will," she whispered. Amanda closed the already small space between them and slipped her arms around his neck and hugged him. "I know it may be crazy. I feel good when I'm with you and..." Colin pulled back slightly and looked in her eyes. She nuzzled up to his warm, strong chest.

"Crazy is sometimes good and worth it." He reached up to tuck a piece of stray hair behind her ear. "I like spending time with you." He smiled. "Now you better walk away before I whisk you off to my house and never let you leave. I'm losing my resolve to be a gentleman."

A mischievous grin crossed Amanda's lips as she patted his chest. "Ok big guy, I'm leaving. Will you promise to kidnap me and lock me in your house for a whole weekend, just you and me?"

His jaw dropped and blinked to clear his thoughts. "I can promise that!"

"You get out of here you rotten boy." She laughed and pushed Colin toward the door. "Talk to you soon!"

"Yes, you will." He trotted down the stairs. *I am in big trouble.* "Bye. Travel safe."

Amanda and Stephanie made the trip back to the city without any incidents. They talked about Colin, Stephanie's kids and her upcoming project that resulted from the weekend. Stephanie took Amanda to her train and shared a tearful goodbye. It never mattered how long they were together, they always seemed to get sad when they had to part ways. With a good hug and a silly joke, Amanda boarded the train and found a seat.

She stowed her bags and nestled into her seat with her book. As she opened to the page she left off on, her phone buzzed from in her purse. After a few moments of searching, the screen was lit with a message.

are you coming home? Brett.

yes honey I should be at the station in 2 hours.

I will meet you there love you Btw heard you had a fun weekend

Damn it Steph. She called Brett to tell him about Colin. I'm going to kill her...

tell you in a bit love you too

Amanda slid her phone back into her bag and pulled her book from her bag. She gazed out the window thinking about how and what she was going to tell Brett when he met her at the station. She smiled at the thought of Colin and worried about what Brett would say. She shook her negative thoughts away and pulled the book open at her book mark. There was a postcard tucked in the spine covering the paragraph on the page. *What is this?* She gently pulled the card out and inspected the picture. It was a crab sitting in the sand with the words: I am crabby when you aren't here. Amanda chuckled at the poor joke but was confused about where it came from. She flipped the card over to see neat printing addressed to her.

Amanda,
You left an impression on me and I can't wait to see you
again.
Colin

Amanda smiled and goose bumps ran up her arms. She quickly pulled her phone out of the bag and searched for Colin's number. She dialed before she lost her nerve and waited for the connection. It rang three times and went to voice mail. She took a deep breath and spoke into the phone.

"Colin, Thank you for the note. It brightened my ride home. I'll talk to you soon."

She pressed end and stared out the window at the passing landscape. The sunlight warmed her face and her eyes closed. Sleep came, allowing her thoughts to rest. Amanda figured she would have time to script what she was going to tell Brett and how she was going to ream out Steph when she got home. Now, she only had 5 minutes before she arrived at the station. *Oh, well! The story that she gave Brett will be close to the truth minus some details. Hopefully he will be fine with Colin.*

"Attention Passengers! Paoli Station is the next stop. Please gather your belongings and get ready to disembark. Thank you for riding with us today and have a great day!" The Announcer said over the loud speaker.

Amanda made sure she had everything she brought and stood by her seat. The train halted and Amanda descended the steps on to the station landing. "Hey Mom!" Brett called through the other passengers.

"Thanks!" Brett took her suitcase and kissed her cheek. "Good to see you. How was your weekend?"

"Nice, I hung out with the guys and worked. Sounds like you had a nice weekend too." He winked.

"Remind me to kill Steph." Amanda mumbled. "Yes I did have a nice weekend. What did she tell you? I need to know where to start."

"She said you met some guy at a party and spent the rest of the weekend with him." He turned to his mom as he loaded the case in the trunk.

"Ok. I met him on the beach when I was out for a run. His dog tackled me. He walked me home from a party and then I spent a day with him. We talked and just spent time together. He knows all about you and your dad. He has three kids and an ex-wife." She breathed after saying all of that without a breath.

"What's his name?"

"Colin."

"Will I meet him sometime?"

"I hope you will. He seems to be a nice guy. He writes for the movie business. I like him." Amanda looked at Brett and saw a look go across his face as if he was about to say something. "No we didn't sleep together." Brett's shoulders relaxed a bit and sighed.

"Sorry Mom! That isn't my business." pretending to cover his ears and block out her words.

She reached over and patted his knee, "This is new territory for both of us and I want to be honest with you. I'll try. Ask if you have concerns." She squeezed his hand and put her hand back on her lap.

~↲~

Back at home, Amanda and Brett fell right back into their normal rhythm. He went to work and hung out with his friends. Amanda busied herself with all the tasks and errands around her house. It had been about a week since her trip to the beach with Stephanie. Amanda was trying not to act like a teenage girl, but was thinking about Colin whenever she had an idle moment. She did text him to let him know she made it home, but hadn't heard from him. Trying not to take it personally or obsess, it was hard to keep those negative thoughts out of an insecure mind. Her inner fifteen year old would occasionally speak up and place doubt in her mind. *I am not going to worry about this. We had a nice time and he lives a different life than me. I am sure that it will work out the way it is supposed to. I am not going to think about Colin anymore!* She went back to cleaning her closet. Clothes were tossed into three piles in Amanda's room. The keep pile, the storage pile and the donate pile. The radio was playing from the hall and Hunter Hayes was singing about wanting something crazy. Amanda was singing quietly while her clothes were flying about the room. The song changed and Amanda kept singing. The house was quiet. The front door slammed.

"Mom? Where are you?"

"Brett...I'm in my room."

"What are you doing?" He asked looking at the mounds of fabrics. He was sweaty and drinking a frosty bottle of soda.

"I'm cleaning. How was your day?" She replied as she climbed out of her closet. When she appeared her hair was wild and her cheeks flushed with the exertion of cleaning.

"So that's what you call this." He laughed and looked about the room. He leaned over the donate pile and kissed her cheek. "My day was good. Do you mind if I go out with the boys tonight?"

"Not at all. I'll be ready to turn in after I am finished cleaning my mess. Will you help me load the donate clothes in the car when I have them bagged?"

"Sure thing! You sure you are ok to have dinner on your own? I can stay."

"No Honey! Please go, enjoy! I'll be good." She reached out and patted his forearm and smiled. "I have pizza in the freezer, a good book and a quiet house. What more could a woman want?" She winked at him.

"Ok. I'll get a shower. I'm meeting the guys at 6." He started down the hall and ducked into his room. "Mom, I'll try to do my closet this week too, ok?"

"That would be great! Thanks Brett!"

"Sure thing," the bathroom clicked closed and the water began running. "Oh Mom! The mail is on the table. You got a letter from New York." The door clicked again and Amanda could hear the faint sounds of Brett singing.

⤳℘ 10 ℈⤳

A letter from New York…losing all control over her fifteen year old self, Amanda dropped the sweater she had in her hand and leaped over the heap of clothes. She slid down the hallway and rounded the corner from the living room to the kitchen. The mail was neatly piled on the table. The magazines were on the bottom, business envelopes in the middle and a beige card shaped envelope on top. *I wonder if is from Colin. Just open it! The front was addressed to Amanda but there was no return address. She flipped it over to look on the back and there was an address but no name.* Amanda took the card from its envelope. The picture was a dune with a setting sun behind it. The inside was covered with neat script reading:

> *Dear Amanda,*
> *Sorry I haven't texted or called since you've been home.*
> *All I have as an excuse is work. I have been thinking of*
> *you often and the time we spent together. I'll try to call*
> *you this week; I have a favor to ask. I also look forward*

to just talking with you. I hope you're well and I will chat
with you soon.
Colin
PS: Toby misses you too.

Amanda smiled and tucked the card back into the envelope.
I wonder what favor he has to ask. Her fifteen year old self was rearing
her head again. Amanda took a deep breath and walked back to her
bedroom to finish her work. *I can listen for the phone and preoccupy*
my mind. So Amanda continued cleaning out her closet and putting
everything back in its place. Brett had left about an hour ago.
Amanda's closet looked organized and tidy. The donation clothes
were bagged and sitting by the front door. The pizza was warming in
the microwave and Amanda was sitting at the table reading through
mail, sipping a glass of water. The microwave timer went off and
Amanda slid the pizza on to a plate and cut it into four slices. As she
ate her third slice, the phone rang. Her heart jumped in the hope that
it was Colin. She looked at the number and smiled, "Hello."

"Hey there! How are you?" His smooth voice slid into her ear
and warmed her heart.

"I'm good, just finishing some dinner. I got your card today.
Thank you! Sorry work has been keeping you so busy." Amanda took
a breath and waited for Colin to answer.

"It's so nice to hear your voice." He sighed and smiled into the
phone. "Work is busy, in a good way but I feel bad that it has taken
so long for us to talk. How was your week?"

"Please don't feel bad. I'm just glad you called, no matter how
long it took. My week has been full of errands and cleaning that
needed to be done."

"Sounds like you were busy too. Do you have plans for the
weekend?" He waited to hear her answer.

"No, not really. Why? Is this your favor?" She smiled and flipped the phone to the other ear.

"Yes, one of them."

"You only mentioned one in your card. You've thought of more things that that you need from me?" with a laugh behind her voice.

"Two more presented themselves today. First, if you're not busy this weekend, would you care to come to a business picnic in the Hamptons? Second, would you like to accompany me to a movie premier on July 1st? The third I will ask you this weekend if you come." He tried to keep his cool while he asked these favors.

"I think I can be of assistance to you on both." She was feeling a bit giddy and excited and was trying to remain calm and collected. "I am a little nervous about number three but I can help you out."

"Really? You'll come this weekend. That's great Amanda! Thank you so much! We can stay at my house...you can have your own room. I can pick you up at the train station and we can ride up together, if that's ok?" He breathed deep again and switched ears.

"That sounds great. Since this is a business picnic, dress is better than shorts and a t-shirt, right?"

"Yes, but shorts are good for anything else we want to do. Would you be able to catch the noon train on Friday?"

"I should be ok. Thanks for asking me. I look forward to seeing you. Do you need me to bring anything special?"

"I'm so glad you can make it. Thank you! Just bring yourself and I will take care of the rest." Colin smiled and had a thought, "will Brett be ok with you coming? I don't want to cause a problem."

"I'm sure he'll be fine but I'll check. If anything changes, I'll text you." Amanda cleared her dinner off the table and placed the mail in the recycling bin and the magazines on the coffee table. While she tidied around the house, they chatted about the week's events.

Conversation flowed and they were both relaxed and laughed with each other.

A phone rang in the background and caused Colin to pause. "Hey Amanda! May I call you back in a bit? I have another call. It's my daughter and I need to talk to her about something."

"Sure thing! I'll be here. Take your time."

"Thanks! I'll call you in a bit." Colin paused and wanted to tell her something else but stopped and hit end.

Amanda finished straightening up and made sure the house was locked. She left a note on the table for Brett and turned the light above the stove on. She headed into her bedroom, went through her night time routine and changed into her pajamas. As she was getting under the covers, the phone rang. She reached for it and turned the TV down. "Hello again."

"Sorry about that. My daughter wanted something and I needed to explain why she can't have it." There was a muffled sound of a bag of chips or something behind him.

"No problem. She ok?"

"She will be. Sometimes she can be a bit spoiled so telling her no is good for her. It keeps her in check, if you know what I mean."

"I understand completely. What are you doing now? It sounds like you're eating or putting away your snack." Amanda snuggled down under the sheet.

"Well, I was putting my dry cleaning away and now I am lying on the couch. What about you, what have you been up to?" Colin slipped his shoes off and pulled off his socks. He loosened the buttons on his shirt and relaxed into the pillows on the couch.

"You sound tired. We can talk later if you want." She frowned at the thought of him hanging up again. She had missed the easy conversation and the soothing sound of his voice. "Although I'd be a little disappointed if you said good night already."

His voice perked up and he spoke directly into the phone. "I'd never disappoint you. I've been looking forward to talking to you for days, so you're not getting rid of me yet. What are you doing now?" He rose from the couch to his bedroom.

"I am tucked into bed with the TV on." She reached for the remote and turned the volume down a bit more.

"So you're in bed right now?" He pulled his shirt off of his chest after he put her on speaker and laid the phone on the bed. "Sounds like a great idea, mind if I join you?"

Amanda blushed and giggled, "You're not going to show up at my door are you?"

"No, although that would be a good idea sometime." He said smoothly.

"Yes, you can join me. What happened to you? You sound far away."

"Sorry. I put you on speaker so I could get ready for bed. Can you give me 2 seconds? I will be right back. Don't go anywhere!" He ducked into the bathroom and came out drying his face and hands. "You still there?"

"You bet! Just waiting for you to tuck me in." sleepily.

"I'm coming." His voice was closer now and just above a whisper. "What do you watch before bed?"

"Usually Friends. Want to watch with me?"

"I would love to." He turned the TV on and searched to find the same channel. He slid between the sheets and rested his head back on the pillows. "I haven't watched it in ages but it's always good for a laugh." His voice relaxed as his body sank into the mattress. He could feel the weight of the day fall from his shoulders.

Amanda could hear him sigh and she felt that ease of conversation flow again. Friends continued in the background while they talked about their kids and what kinds of things were happening at work for

Colin. His voice was low and sweet and she thought about how easily she could fall asleep listening to him. "Do you read?" She blurted out.

"I can read if that's what you're asking." He chuckled.

"No... I assumed you could read but do you like to?"

"I used to read a lot but I haven't in ages. Why?"

"You're going to think I'm silly." She paused to think about what to say next and Colin didn't interrupt. "I was listening to you and was thinking that your voice would be great for bedtime stories. Did you read to your kids? If not they missed out." She nervously rambled.

"I have to say no one has ever said that to me. And yes, I did read to my kids. I was pretty good at it too." He smiled. "I will have to remember that when you come up this weekend. I might have to have my assistant run out to Barnes and Noble to get some books. Any requests?" He joked.

"Stop teasing! I was giving you a compliment and you are making fun." She giggled and pulled the sheet over her head shyly.

"I'm not teasing, I'm flattered. Thank you. By the way, your voice is not bad to listen to either. I'm certain your students love listening to you read. You probably do the voices too." He was teasing but was so happy to have her to talk to.

"Ok. Change the subject. What time do you need to get up in the morning? I'm not keeping you up past your bed time, am I?"

"No," he said yawning. "I'm fine." Sleep was tempting his mind and eye lids.

"Colin, you sound exhausted. Go to sleep. I'll talk to you later. Don't forget I'll see you Friday."

"I don't want to say good night, yet." He pouted. "I like talking to you and I want to hear your voice," he stomped his feet under the covers.

"I'm glad that you like talking to me. I like talking to you. You're tired and we have ALL weekend to talk. Please go to sleep. I'll tuck you in, get some rest, ok?"

"Ok... I'll go to bed." Colin conceded, pouting. He knew he needed some sleep. "I'll rest now so we can have lots of talk time over the weekend. Thanks again for coming. I'm looking forward to it."

"Me too! Good night Colin. Sleep well and I'll see you soon." Amanda whispered into the phone. She smiled as she tucked him in and was ready to hang up the phone when she heard him whisper back.

"Night Amanda! Sweet dreams." Colin gently pressed end and burrowed into the pillow.

11

$\mathcal{F}$riday had finally arrived. Amanda was walking up the platform to the train. She smiled as she thought of Brett and telling him she was going to see Colin for the weekend. He was happy and even took a couple of hours off from work to take her to the station.

"Have fun Mom. Call if you need anything. I'll be working and hanging with the boys, usual stuff. Scott wanted to go fishing so we'll do that Sunday morning." He pulled her into a hug before he got back in the car. "I love you. Have a good time. Don't do anything I wouldn't do." He backed toward the car and winking and laughing.

"Thanks! See you Sunday. I love you. Take care and you stay out of trouble too." She winked and waved back.

The sun was warm and the train was arctic. Amanda pulled a sweatshirt and book from her bag. Trees were swaying as the train glided along the tracks. Summer was gearing up to be a hot one. June was early in the season but it was becoming a sweltering month. As she was daydream out the window, her phone chirped.

Hey are you on the train Texted Colin.

Yes about an hour away.

Great meet you at the station.

See you soon

Can't wait

Amanda smiled and tried to keep from bouncing out of her seat. She was hoping for the best weekend. She was nervous that Colin would be everything she remembered him to be.

~ℓ⌓~

Amanda anxiously tapped her foot for the train to stop in the station. Her heart fluttered at the thought of seeing Colin in a matter of minutes. Insecurity erupted in her thoughts and she quickly pushed it back under the surface. Amanda knew that her life was nowhere near as busy as his. It was dull and mundane compared to Colin's existence. She continued to nervously rub her hands and fidget in her seat.

"Ladies and Gentlemen, thank you for riding with us today. We are settling into the station. You'll hear the doors open shortly. Have a great day!" The announcer said kindly over the speaker.

Amanda took two deep breaths and hastily gathered her things. She rose from the seat aware of her excitement, trying to keep it in check. Her steps were brisk on the platform and racing closer to the stairs. Her heart was beating in rhythm with her shoes on the concrete floor. She took deep breaths to try to slow it down. She reached the top of the stairs scanning for Colin. Her eyes moved around and she was getting an uneasy feeling. Her heart was tightening... her phone was buzzing.

Behind you beautiful

Amanda turned with warmth rushing to her cheeks. Clear green eyes were smiling at her and two strong arms pulled her into a hug. "Hey you!" She said letting out the breath she was holding and fell into his embrace. "So nice to see you."

Colin smiled and inhaled her lavender and fabric softener scent. "I'm so glad you're here. It felt like forever. Good trip?"

Amanda nodded against his chest. He smelled like city and fresh linen. She pulled back and smiled at him. "Quiet trip. How was your morning?"

"Morning was good. I had a few meetings and a few errands to run before I needed to come to the train station to pick up my weekend date." He grinned and reached for her bag. "Come on pretty lady, my car is back at my apartment. We will grab a cab and head there so I can grab my stuff. You don't mind seeing my place before we head out?" he asked.

"Not at all. Lead the way!" He reached for her hand and took her out into the warm summer light. "What's our plan today?" She nervously inquired.

He opened the door to the cab in front of them at the busy curb, "Well, I was thinking we'd have dinner on the porch and watch the sun set...sound ok?" He slid closed to her on the hot, black vinyl seat.

"Sounds perfect. Where is Toby?"

"He is here in the city. He will ride up with us. He has been talking about you nonstop. He is so excited to run with you on the beach. I can't shut him up." Colin reached into his pocket for the fare. They were still a couple of blocks away.

Amanda smiled and laughed lightly. She gazed out into the busy city street. *Keep breathing. He is happy to see you. Relax and enjoy your time and company. Let your guard down and have fun!* Amanda scolded herself. Colin reached over and brushed his fingers over her knee.

"You ok?" His eyes full of concern.

She nodded and smiled reassuringly. "Yes, trying to catch my breath," holding his hand on her knee.

"You don't have to stay if it's too much too soon. I would understand, be disappointed, but understand." Giving her hand a light squeeze.

She squeezed back. "No Colin, I'm glad to be here. I'm glad to be here with you." She stopped to check his face and continued, "Thank you for inviting me for the weekend." She smiled at him, hoping he understood what she was not so eloquently trying to say.

As he was going to slide closer to her, the cab stopped in front of his building. He slipped the driver the cash and opened the door to get out. Amanda stepped from the cab and followed Colin into the building. He greeted the door man and said, "Bernie, this is Amanda."

"Nice to meet you Miss Amanda." Bernie took her hand to shake. "Please let me know if you need anything, while you're here."

"Thanks Bernie. It's very nice to meet you." Amanda smiled warmly and turned after Colin. He was holding the button for the elevator. Amanda stepped in and Colin was behind her. The doors closed and she could feel his eyes on her. She stole a look at him and he was staring into her eyes.

As he placed her bag on the floor and stood toe to toe with her. He drew in the scent of her and began, "I want you to know that I feel honored that you're here with me. I don't date and I am scared of what might come from us being together." He tenderly touched her cheek and kissed her lightly on the mouth. "You're a beautiful person that I am very excited and intrigued to learn more about. Just promise me that you will talk to me and tell me if you need a break or anything." He looked deeply into her eyes and held her gaze as he kissed her forehead. "Deal?"

Amanda sighed and leaned forward to hug him. "Thank you. I'll tell you anything, as long as you will do the same. Deal?"

"Deal." He hugged her back and kissed the top of her forehead. The doors opened and they both walked out of the elevator. He led her out of the elevator and toward his apartment door. "Welcome. Toby will be very excited to see you, prepare yourself. I have to say that his manners are no better than they were a few weeks ago. Although we have been practicing." Colin unlocked the door.

Amanda could hear his paws on the floor before she saw him through the doorway. "Hey Toby! How's my favorite dog?" Amanda knelt on the floor right inside the front door and rubbed Toby's ears.

"How about I go grab my stuff while you two get reacquainted?" He walked down the hall. Seconds later, Toby padded down the hall after him. "What done already? You have been pacing impatiently for days and now you left her alone in the foyer."

"No, he is giving me a tour." Amanda walked into his room and sat on the bed. "Since his human was all business and wanted to get out of the city." She laughed. Toby jumped on to the bed and nuzzled up to Amanda's legs.

"Well… it was all part of my plan to get you in my bedroom on my bed." He leaned toward her with a mischievous twinkle in his eyes. "Thank Toby! You are my best friend." Colin fist bumped his paw and then walked to the bathroom to gather the rest of his things. When he came back, Amanda was no longer on his bed. He regretted the flirting that he had just done, fearing he scared her away. "Amanda?"

"In the kitchen. I am getting some water. You want anything?" She reached into the bare fridge to see water bottles and beer. The eggs were a bit lonely in the door.

"Water would be great, thanks! Make yourself at home. What's mine is yours." He appeared in the hall with his bag. His face was relieved to find her looking out the window over the city. He walked over to her. "You look great in my apartment." He smoothly slid his hand around her waist pulling her away from the window.

"Do you know how irresistible you are?" She curved into his chest and put her empty hand around him. "I have a feeling we are going to be in big trouble this weekend. We almost were in trouble in your room a few minutes ago." She batted her eyelashes.

He sighed realizing she was feeling the attraction too. They were both gun shy but could not deny the pull they had on each other. "I hate to tell you but you're pretty irresistible yourself." He brushed a kiss across her smiling lips. "Now, let's get out of here and go to the beach. We can relax and enjoy a little get away. We can always come back here later if we need to." He said reaching for Toby's leash. "I want to take you away from all this and have you all to myself."

The ride to the beach house was full of laughter and barks, Colin turned on the radio and began singing along. Amanda refused to let him sing alone, so she joined in on the melodies. Toby thought they were calling the dogs so he howled along too. By the time they pulled into the drive way, their faces hurt from all the smiling and laughing. Amanda quickly texted Brett and told him she was there and things were good.

Colin carried the bags and things into the house. Amanda and Toby followed on his heels. "Would you mind opening some windows and the back door down here? I'll get the ones upstairs." She nodded in response and walked through the house unlocking and lifting the sashes. After he finished up stairs, he called through the house, "Amanda?" He heard no reply so he walked toward the porch. He found her sitting on the first step watching Toby meander through the dunes. "How you doin'?" doing his best Joey voice. He sat down beside her.

She rubbed her arms as if she were cold, it was 80 degrees. "I am great! Just watching him sniff and check things out. I don't often think about how I miss having a dog. They are so easy to please. I get so envious of their simple life." She said leaning against the railing.

"I never thought of that. You're right. He's happy with just about anything and gets so excited about the small things." Colin sat reflecting on these true thoughts and the peacefulness of the moment. "Would you like anything to drink? I have to run to the store, you can stay or come along." He looked at her beauty, it was quiet but confident. *What a lucky guy I am to be sitting next to her.*

"Would you mind if I take a bath and freshen up while you go?"

"Not at all. Do you have any special requests? Cream for coffee or anything?"

"I'll need cream and sugar. Surprise me with anything else." She smiled at him and stood.

"Go enjoy a hot bath. I'll be back shortly. Your bag is on the bed in the blue room at the top of the stairs." He reached over and brought her hand to his lips. She turned to the house and called Toby. Colin fished his keys out of his pocket and walked to the Rover. He turned when he heard his name from the house.

"Colin, thank you for…" She paused. She was unsure what she wanted to thank him for, everything, time, attention, affection…

His grin shone from the driveway. "My pleasure."

12

Amanda drew a hot bath in the antique claw foot tub. She had put clothes on the bed to change into and slipped into the soothing water. As she closed her eyes to reflect on the day she felt herself smile. Colin was being a nice, understanding guy. He knew she was nervous about a new relationship but still wanted to be with him. She knew that his divorce hurt him and he was afraid to get too close. They both had their issues but they still enjoyed each other's company and had a connection that allowed them to feel something for each other.

Time passed and she drifted into a light nap. As her consciousness slipped away, Todd came to her thoughts. He was sitting on the toilet watching her take a bath. He used to love coming in and talking to her while she bathed. It was one time that they were truly alone.

"Honey, why are you dreaming about me?" His voice startled her.

"I am worried I am betraying you somehow." She dreamed. "I loved you for so long and now you're gone. I was unprepared. I don't want you to think that I loved you less than I do...did...do." She whispered confused.

"Amanda, I love you still and I want you to be happy. If you want to be with Colin, then do it. I know that you still love me and that will never change. Please don't sacrifice your happiness on my memory. I'm here with you and I will watch over you. Fall in love or not, but you have to know what your heart is telling you."

"Todd! I miss you every day. You were my best friend, the father of my son and my husband. I wish you could meet him and tell me what you think. I think you and Colin would have liked each other." A tear ran down her cheek from her dreaming eyes.

"I trust your opinion of him and I am watching to make sure he takes care of my girl. I love you sweetie." As he uttered the last four words, the vision of him left the bathroom like steam on the mirror.

Amanda blinked her eyes and wiped the tears from her face with the back of her hand, "I love you." The water was beginning to chill. Amanda pulled the chain on the plug and wrapped herself in an oversized blue towel. There were voices and footsteps downstairs, Colin must be back. She dried quickly and dressed for the evening in jeans and a loose t-shirt. Her hair was combed and laying on her back. Before heading to the kitchen, she hung the towel and put her worn clothes in the basket in the bathroom.

The voices were singing not talking and they were coming from the stereo in the living room. Colin was singing as he put the food in the cabinets and fridge. He stopped and took a sip of the beer on the counter. When he went to put the bottle down, he caught a glimpse of Amanda watching him from the door. A smile spread across his face and he held out his hand as a slow song came from the speakers. Amanda slipped her hand into his and walked closer to his chest, where she rested her head as he swayed them to the music. He smelled her hair and kissed her forehead. "Good bath?"

"Relaxing. Toby didn't even bother me. I thought he might sit by the tub and wait for me."

"Nah, he is afraid you will put him in. He doesn't like the tub. He is more of a shower dog." They continued to dance around the kitchen. "I ordered pizza. Cheese ok? It'll be here in 20."

She took in the scent of him on his shirt and sighed. "Perfect." She reached her hands around his neck and pulled his face to hers. They kissed softly and danced just a little closer. "Could I have a beer too? Yours tastes good," as she licked the flavor from her lips.

"You bet." He stepped to the fridge and pulled one from the shelf, twisted the top and handed it to her. "My lady."

"Thank you sir." She took a swallow and looked into his green eyes. They were looking at her with an intensity that made her knees go weak. She looked over his shoulder at the remaining food to be put away. "Would you care for some help?"

"Sure, but only if you save me another dance." Those smoldering eyes were twinkling too. He spun her out across the kitchen when she nodded her reply.

~ℓ⅃~

The pizza arrived and they sat on the back porch to eat. The sun was beginning to set. The sky was ablaze with orange, purple and pink. They both seemed to be staring at the same thing and Toby broke the silence. "Ok buddy. Let's go look at this beautiful sunset on the beach. What do you say?" He offered his hand to Amanda.

"Sounds great!"

The clouds were fluffy, purples and oranges. The water was reflecting the beautiful pastels while lapping up on the shore. Toby chased his tennis ball into the surf and ran back to Amanda willing to play more. Colin's long fingers were laced with Amanda's non-throwing hand. He chuckled every time Toby came running with his tongue hanging out the side of his mouth. *Amanda was such a great "dog person". She had a way with Toby and people. I know it is too early for her to meet my kids but I want them to like her as much as I do. I wonder what her son is like. I hope he would like me. I will have to ask more about Brett to find out what kind of kid he is.* He was pondering through his thoughts when he noticed his hand was empty.

"Penny for your thoughts?" Amanda was sitting in the sand with Toby chewing on a stick he found. She was looking at him with her chocolate brown eyes full of curiosity.

"I was wondering if Brett would like me. Not that it's important right now but I would like you to meet my kids sometime. Maybe you and Brett could come up and spend a few days while the kids are here? Would you like that?"

"Is that the third thing you wanted to ask me?"

"Um… no but I… no, I am not asking yet. And you can't make me."

"Really?" she replied raising her eyebrows. She leaned closer to him, almost touching his face and smiled slyly. "I have no way of getting you to reveal your secret question?" She began to run your fingers over his ribs and he jerked away. At that movement, she went in for the full tickle attack. Colin fell back in the sand laughing and flailing at her quick hands.

"Stop… can't… breathe… please… no… tickling… too much…" Amanda was retreating when he lunged at her to get her ribs. A look as satisfaction crossed his face when she fell back.

"You're a cheater!" she gasped. She grabbed his shirt front and pulled him closer. She kissed him. It caught him off guard and fell into her mouth. His body relaxed into her without all of his body weight on her. "I win!" She laughed between kisses.

"You're the cheater. You just took advantage of me." He gave her a sexy smile with the heat from his eyes penetrating her soul. He liked being this close to her but knew that if he didn't get up now;

things might get too hot for the beach. Colin sat down beside her and offered a hand to pull her into a seated position. "Sorry."

"What are you sorry for? I started it." She looked down at the sand with an ashamed look on her face. She took a deep breath and looked up into his green eyes. "Colin, we like each other. We're attracted to each other. I don't want to go too fast but I also can't deny the way you make my body respond to you." She reached over to his cheek and brushed sand away. Her face was shy but there was intensity in her eyes.

Colin didn't realize that he was looking at her with an open mouth. He snapped his jaw shut and shook his head. "I feel like we're connected somehow. I guess I worry about you, thinking I invited you here to jump into bed with you. I'm *not* that guy."

Amanda crawled toward him to end up between his legs. She pulled her eyes up to his and rested her hands on his shoulders. "I trust you didn't invite me here to have your way with me, but I also look forward to us having our way with each other, whenever that happens. Also, if you think you're going to treat me like a cheap slut, I'll kick your ass. Got it?" She lightly pressed her palms to the sides of his face and smiled lightly.

Colin grinned and relaxed at her touch and words. "I'm so glad I joined you by the fire that night. I felt like a moth being drawn to a flame. You warm my heart and I look forward to being with you. But…"

She leaned in to kiss him and as she did Toby pressed his nose right in between their faces.

"Toby! You know how to ruin a moment!" They both laughed and stood to walk back to the house.

~ℓↄ~

Colin and Amanda cleaned up the dinner dishes and pizza box and set up the coffee pot for morning. Toby napped on the rug by the back door. The music from the stereo was competing with the night creatures outside. Colin turned to say something to Amanda and she was no longer in the kitchen. He hung the towel in the oven door and walked toward the living room. She was looking at family pictures on the wall with a quiet thoughtful look about her. He leaned into her ear and whispered, "What's going on in that pretty head? You're awful quiet."

"Do you miss being a family?" She whispered before she could stop herself.

His brow furrowed and then he nodded slightly. "I miss being in the same house with my kids every day, but I don't miss my ex. We were not happy and that made coming home miserable. I would look forward to when she would be away and it would be just me and the kids. Don't get me wrong, Shelly is a great mom but we were not a good couple anymore."

Amanda leaned against him and sighed. "I hope they know what a great dad they have."

"Pat and David are wonderful boys and are understanding of what Shelly and I went through. Tiffani... she thinks I am the bad guy most of the time." His thoughts took him away to his kids. A smile crossed his face. "We, Shelly and I tried to keep things civil and peaceful for the kids. So far they are ok. That's why we share the beach house. We have so many memories here together; we didn't want to end that, even if one of us wasn't here with them all the time." He smiled again and ran his hands on Amanda's upper arms.

"I'm so glad that you two can still be friendly after all that you have been through. My kids at school have gone through *ugly* divorces and I feel so bad for them. They have no idea what kind of love and respect makes a marriage or relationship work." She frowned at the memory of some of her students coming to school crying or depressed every day because of the drama their parents were bringing them into.

Both Amanda and Colin were standing reflecting on their families and thoughts when they both yawned. "I think I will take Toby out before bed." Colin said with a stretch.

"I think I am going to turn in. Thanks for this weekend time with you." She gave him a kiss on the cheek and turned toward the stairs. He turned to take Toby out. "Good night. Sleep well."

"See you in the morning."

Amanda was lying on crisp, cool sheets in the light blue room. Thoughts were racing through her mind about Colin. *What he was doing? Is he asleep? I wonder if he is having a good time. What will we do in the morning? Will I be able to run in the morning?* She huffed and rolled over to try to go to sleep. *This is ridiculous. I am never going to fall asleep and then I will look horrible tomorrow and his friends and colleagues will think I am old and haggard. I need to do something. What?* Amanda threw the covers back and walked to the window. The moonlight was reflecting off of the water and there was a light knock at the door. Did I really hear that? "Colin?"

"Are you ok?" His voice was just a whisper from outside the door. The door creaked slightly and his kind green eyes peeked in at her.

"I'm ok. Just can't sleep. You?"

"Me either. You want to talk or some warm milk or something?"

Amanda thought for a moment and walked over to the door. Words were not coming to her and ideas of what to do were not coming. She felt like a deer in the headlights.

Colin pushed the door open and reached for her hand. Without saying a word, led her to his room, pulled back the covers and motioned for her to get in. He walked to the opposite side and crawled under the sheet. Finally breaking the silence, "How about we try this?" His was eyeing Amanda with a look of understanding and lay on his back looking at the ceiling.

"I am starting to think you can read my mind. You can't right?" She gave him a questioning look.

"NO! I wish! Then I wouldn't have to wonder what you're thinking and feeling." He sighed and relaxed into the mattress.

Amanda rolled onto her side and looked at his beautiful moon lite profile. She brushed her fingers lightly across his check and whispered, "Thank you for being you and knowing what I need even when I don't." Her body was giving into sleep. Her eyes were getting heavy. "Night Colin."

He turned his head to see her eyes go closed. "Sleep well Amanda." His heart was falling for this woman and he was scared. So many things felt perfect with her and he felt whole and at peace with her close. He wanted to wrap his arms around her but wanted her to sleep without being spooked by him. Before he could stop himself words escaped his lips, "I love you."

"I love you," she whispered. And with that Colin fell into dream land with his heart full and hopeful.

13

The sun was peeking through the blinds, warming the room in yellows and blues. Colin reached for Amanda and her side of the bed was empty. He pried his sleepy eyes open and tried to figure out if it was a dream. *Did she sleep in my bed? Why did she run away? I hope I didn't scare her off last night. That was the best sleep I've had in a long time. I wonder where she is.* He climbed out of her side of the bed and walked down the hall. Toby was waiting at the bottom of the stairs with a satisfied look on his face. "What, you crazy dog?"

The smell of coffee was wafting through the first floor. Colin scanned the kitchen and there was no activity except for the brewing coffee maker. Toby looked at Colin and walked over to the screen door. "Do you need to go out?" Toby sat down as if to say no.

Colin poured himself a mug full of coffee and walked out to the back porch. He looked over the quiet beach and saw a figure sitting in the sand with her back facing him. "Toby, is that what you're trying to tell me? Does she have coffee?" *I can't believe I just asked the dog and expected and answer.* Colin breezed into the kitchen to fix her coffee. As he headed toward the door, he looked down at his bare

chest. *Guess I should get dressed.* He grabbed a sweatshirt from behind
the door and began his trek to the beach.

He slid beside her and held out the coffee mug. "I hope I did ok."

She smiled sliding the mug from his warm hand. "Thanks. It
looks perfect." Amanda took a cautious sip. "You nailed it. Thanks!"
She leaned toward him and bumped his shoulder. "Sorry I snuck
out. I went for a run." She smiled apologetically. "Running always
clears my head."

"You needed to clear your head?" Colin probed. He tilted his
head toward her, hoping for a heart spilling conversation.

Amanda looked into his eyes, there was a mischievous twinkle.
She warmly smiled and reached for his hand. "You know exactly why
I needed to think. Don't you worry that we're moving too fast?" Her
voice slipped to just above a whisper.

Colin turned toward her and looked into her eyes. "Amanda.
I'm sorry I said what I did last night. I wasn't trying to scare you or
make you uncomfortable. I was feeling it. It slipped out. If you're
rethinking your choice of staying this weekend, I understand. I can
take you home. Please don't do anything you don't want to." He
shifted in the sand in a wave of sadness and uncertainty.

Amanda saw the emotions travel across his face. She got to her
feet and pulled him to his. "Listen Colin, I'm not scared of what you
said or spending time with you. I am afraid of the short time that
we have known each other and the swiftness of all of these feelings.
I trust you." With that said she stepped up and kissed him. It was
soft and loving at first, becoming more lustful. Amanda let out a
soft moan and whispered between kisses, "Colin, if you remember,
I said it back to you last night." She laughed and pulled away from
him. "Let's eat some breakfast." She led him back to the house with
Toby in tow.

14

"Are you ready?" Colin called up the stairs.

She appeared from the bedroom. The sun was making her white cotton dress glow and her hair was hanging on her left shoulder.

"Wow! You look beautiful. I don't think I want to share you with anyone else tonight." He bounded up the stairs, swept her up into his arms and walked them both back into the bedroom.

"Stop it!" Slapping him gently on the chest and laughing at his thought. "You have business to take care of and I have to hang on your every word like the arm candy I am." She said putting a wisp of his hair in place.

"You are my partner tonight not my arm candy. While I'm talking business you may stay with me or mingle. I want you to have a good time and if you're ready to go, I want you to tell me. I go when you go. Got it? This is our time."

"Got it!" She kissed him on the cheek and grabbed her light sweater off the hook by the door. "Are we walking or driving?" She said resting her hand on the door knob.

"I never know what to expect from you. As soon as I think I know, you surprise me. Thank you for that, by the way. I've missed surprises in my life and you are the best surprise ever!" He slipped his arm around her waist and led her out the door. "Driving, so I can bring you home whenever we're ready to escape the snobbery and business functions."

The house was huge. Trees and flowers surrounded the driveway and there were tiki torches flaming along the walkway. The sun was still blazing its trail down toward the horizon. A warm breeze was coming from the ocean and both Colin and Amanda were feeling nervous. He was nervous about what was going to happen when they got back to the house. He was hoping that something special could happen. Amanda was nervous about making a good impression and making Colin proud. They both exhaled a breath that they didn't know they were holding as they walked toward the music pouring from the pool area.

Colin slipped his fingers between hers and pulled her closer to him as they approached the other guests. "Thank you for being here. Please let me know if you're not having a good time." He whispered in her ear and then lightly kissed her hair.

Amanda looked into his eyes and nodded. She was afraid to say anything but was so glad to be holding his hand. It was very calming. They both walked toward a group of people standing and sitting around a fountain. They were laughing and chatting about a book they had all read. A red head was saying that it was horrible, far-fetched and lacked excitement. The blonde man standing across from her argued by saying it was futuristic and full of human emotion. Just because there were no gunfights and killing doesn't mean it was missing excitement, he retorted. Amanda was soaking it in, when Colin's voice pulled her from the words.

"Good afternoon everyone! What a beautiful day to see you all here." He said smiling at his colleagues and shaking hands. "I hope you haven't made any decisions without me."

"No, of course not. You're our best idea man and we can't do this without you," sang a little, young woman with cream colored skin and bright blue eyes. She stepped toward Colin and slid next him on the opposite side of Amanda. She was giving a skeptical look to Amanda and wiggling closer to Colin.

Amanda was watching this young woman and wondering who she was. Colin didn't seem to notice her or the proximity of her vibrant body. As Amanda was puzzling over this young woman, Colin introduced her to the men and women standing in the group. Everyone was very friendly and warm as they were nodding or shaking her hand. The red headed woman from the book conversation shook her hand and said that she had heard so much about her in the past few weeks. Her name was Margie; she shared an office with Colin. They were friends and had known each other in college. The introductions ended and conversations continued and started anew. Both Amanda and Colin spoke and enjoyed the relaxed dialogue that was happening.

"Would you like a drink?"

"Yes, please." She took his offered hand and followed him to the bar by the pool. "Who is the young lady that was beside you?" Amanda asked curiously.

"Who? Oh, Candy… she is an intern from Columbia." He reached for the two beers and handed one to Amanda. "Why do you ask?"

"She likes you. Maybe even wants to be closer to you than just an intern in the office."

"Yeah, right! I am old enough to be her father." He shook his head in disbelief.

"I may be wrong, but just be careful. She has that look in her eyes for you."

"I don't think I need to worry, but I will be careful. Thanks. You ok?"

"Yes I'm fine. They all seem very nice and they respect you very much. I didn't realize how important you are to the business."

"I'm not that important but thanks for saying so. I like my work and I like most of the people I work with. I just wish I didn't work as much as I do. I would like more time with my family to do fun things, like kayaking or traveling."

"I hope that you can find time to do those things. Family is important and enjoying life is important too." Amanda touched her hand to his chest and smiled at him. "If you don't enjoy life, what's the point?"

As Colin was about to speak, a voice interrupted. "Colin, could you help Max and Ben settle a debate? They are fighting about which leading lady is better to play the part of Jane" Candy smiled sweetly at Amanda as she lead Colin back to the circle. Colin looked back at Amanda and she nodded for him to go.

As he talked with his business partners, Amanda walked around the pool and watched the sun get closer to the horizon. She reflected quietly on Colin and the relationship they were creating. *He is a wonderful man and he seemed to have the best intentions. What would Stephanie say to all of this?* Amanda wanted to have an outside opinion and was about to pull out her phone and walk down to the beach for some privacy, when that voice trilled behind her. "What are you doing here with him? He is so out of your league." Candy was smugly smiling at Amanda.

"Pardon me? What are you talking about?" Amanda's defenses went up and she was rigid with anger.

"You're just a teacher and have no idea what kind of world Colin lives and works in. Why don't you just stay in Pennsylvania and let me take care of him?"

"I'm not sure who you are but you have no right to be speaking to me this way or about something that is none of your business. Excuse me!" Amanda tried to walk calmly past Candy and back to the buzzing party. She scanned the crowd for Colin and he waved to her from the stairs beyond the pool. She drew in a breath and navigated through the crowd toward Colin. He met her halfway and hugged her.

"You alright?" He pulled away from her and looked lovingly into her eyes. He could see that something had upset her but wasn't sure what could have happened with all of these people that were strangers to her. "What happened?" He hugged her again, she was shaking.

"Could you please take me back to the house or call me a cab." She snapped and instantly felt horrible. The look on his face was worry, hurt and confusion. "I can't talk right now. I am too angry and don't want to say something that I will regret or be unfair to someone. Please let me go back to the house. I will go alone and let you finish your work. Please!" She pleaded.

"What happened?" Colin pulled back and got his keys from his pocket. "I'll take you back to the house." He slid his hand into hers.

"Colin, please don't leave if you have more to do. I can take a cab. I should take some time for myself anyway, to cool down." She whispered to him.

"I will take you home and if you are sure that you're alright, I will come back to finish up some things. Are you sure you don't want to talk?"

"Truly, I'll be fine alone for a bit. I need to cool down."

"Will you tell me what happened?" a look of concern in his eyes.

"Maybe later. Please just take me back to your house." She was still shaking and couldn't look in his eyes.

With their hands laced together, they walked down the path

to the car. He drove her home and tried to calm his worry as she quietly gazed out the window at the passing houses. He pulled up to the front of the house and walked around to help her out of the car. As she slid out of the seat and her feet met the gravel below, she reached up to his moonlit face. "Thanks. I will take care of Toby. You go back and finish your business." She looked into his eyes and sighed. He looked so worried and afraid of what was going on with her. "I'll be here when you get back. We can talk then." She kissed his cheek and walked toward the front door.

"You'll need this." He said tossing her the keys. She unlocked the door and then tossed them back. "I will be an hour. Go take a long bath and I will see you when I get back." He smiled a weak smile and began to walk to the driver's side of the car. He waved as he pulled out and Amanda closed the door behind her.

After she let Toby out, she walked up the stairs to the bedroom and pulled pajamas from her bag. She went to the bathroom and took a quick hot shower to rinse the anger off. *How could that young chippy talk to her like she owned a man that was old enough to be her father? She doesn't know me or our relationship but felt entitled to control Colin's love life. I can't believe her and how angry she made me. I was ready to slap her and I'm not sure why I got so angry. She just pissed me off!*

Amanda put on her cool cotton pajamas and walked to the kitchen for some tea. Then went to the couch to continue to ponder Candy's motives. As she sat thinking with Toby cuddled up beside her, she dozed off.

"Hey pretty lady! Rough night?" a familiar voice said to her.

"Todd? What are you doing here?" Amanda questioned him.

"I'm checking on my girl. That girl was just being a bitch. Don't let her change your mind about Colin. He really cares for you."

"I know I shouldn't be angry but it struck a nerve. Should I tell him what happened? I don't want to cause a problem for him at work."

Todd nodded. "Tell him. My guess is he already knows. You keep talking to him and be honest. You two are happier together, than apart."

"Todd, why are you being a matchmaker? It's weird!" Amanda said smiling at him.

"You need to be happy and I am enjoying watching you find happiness. You deserve it. I love you, honey!"

"I love you and I miss you every day." Amanda choked out.

"I know sweetie, but you need to move on. Colin is the man to help you do that and you are the woman to help him. Talk to him when he gets home."

"I will. I promise."

He smiled and slowly faded away.

Amanda felt warm fingers brushing her hair away from her face and smiled. *Am I still dreaming?* Her eyes fluttered open and saw Colin kneeling in front of her. She smiled and touched the scruff along his jawline. "You're home."

"How you doing? Feeling better?" His voice was soft and his eyes were warm and patient.

"Yes. I'm not telling you to make a big deal of things or to make trouble. I want you to know. Ok?" Amanda pulled herself up to a seated position and Toby growled as she moved and disturbed him. She chuckled as she reached down to rub his head. "Sorry buddy."

Colin crossed his legs and stayed on the floor. He looked up at her face as she took a deep breath. He could tell that she was nervous about what she was about to tell him. He reached for her hand and rubbed it with his thumb. He nodded for her to start when she was ready.

Ok, here it goes. Amanda took in a deep breath and looked into his calm green eyes. "I was looking out over the water and enjoying the view while you were talking with your colleagues. I was content. Candy came down behind me and began talking to me. She told me that I have no right to be with you because I'm not from the same world that you're from. She made it clear that I need to go home." Silent tears ran down Amanda's cheeks as she told the story. "I was so caught off guard that my defenses went up and I said she had no right to speak me that way or about things that were none of her business." She drew in another breath and looked at Colin. "I'm sorry I lost my cool. I don't know what came over me but I was pissed and I needed to get away from her before I slapped her. I didn't want to do that in front of all of those people. I didn't want to embarrass you."

Colin was still looking at her but he was now holding both of her hands in his. He sat up on his knees so they were face to face. "Please don't ever apologize for your feelings. You were right to be angry. Candy crossed a line tonight and I have no intention of letting her tell you to go away. I'm a big boy and know that I want you to stay." He smiled and brushed a tear from her cheek. "Don't give her a second thought, but if she ever says an unkind word to you again, you have my permission to slap her. She needs to know her place in my life, which is as an intern at the office and nothing else." He slid his hands into Amanda's hair and tilted her face too his. He leaned down and kissed her. It was gentle and loving at first. Then Amanda's hands tangled in Colin's hair and want and desire were screaming through her kiss.

While catching their breath, she rested her head on his shoulder and snuggled even closer to him. He reached up to brush the hair away from her face and kissed the top of her head. "Come on. Let's go to bed. Tomorrow is our last day together and I want to enjoy you well rested and relaxed." He wrapped his arm around her waist and led her upstairs. She stopped at her room to brush her teeth and came to his room. Colin pulled the covers back and guided her to lie down. He tucked the sheet and blanket around her. He walked to the bathroom and readied himself for bed. The mattress lowered as his body settled down for the night. He nestled under the sheet and sighed into the pillow. "Colin." Amanda whispered.

"Yes."

"May I... would you mind..."

"Come over here." He pulled her over beside him and she rested her head on his chest. He lightly traced his fingers over her bare shoulder and felt the goose bumps rise on her skin.

"Thank you. I need you... I mean I need to be close to you. That sounds... crazy I guess. It has been an interesting night and you make me feel calmer and safe."

He gave her a little squeeze and smiled into the dark bedroom. "I am glad to hear you say that. I was feeling the same way. I sleep better with you in my arms. I love having you beside me. You are a wonderful woman and... I'm falling in love with you." He shook his head and continued with his declaration, "Now go to sleep before I say anything else."

Amanda lifted her head from his chest and leaned toward his lips. Her eyes met his and she held her breath. She could see the adoration in his eyes and kissed him with the love she had growing for him. Their lips were soft and warm as they met. Colin and Amanda smiled at one another. "Good night sweet Colin." Amanda whispered as she rested her head back on his chest. Both Colin and Amanda's breathing slowed and they drifted off to sleep.

15

Sunday had arrived. Colin and Amanda were still tangled together in bed. The sun's rays peeked through the blinds. Colin snuggled closer to Amanda. He lightly kissed the back of her head and slipped carefully out of bed. He tiptoed down the stairs to the kitchen. He began the coffee and put some bread in the toaster. Just as he was loading the tray to carry it up to Amanda, he felt two arms around his waist. He froze in place as she placed a kiss on his bare neck. "Morning handsome!"

His breath caught. He turned. Her eyes were soft with sleep and her hair was pulled into a messy bun on the nape of her neck. "You look beautiful this morning. How do you…" Just as he was about to finish his sentence, she stretched up to press her lips to his. The passion in her action was overwhelming. He lifted her to rest on the counter. His hands were on her hips and then her back. His heart was racing mirroring hers pounding against her chest. His hands wrapped around the back of her neck and pulled gently at the bun in her hair. As his lips traveled to her neck and ears, he whispered, "What are you doing to me?"

She panted. She tried catching her breath. Then looked into his gorgeous eyes. They still had a bit of sleep in them but had a slow burn of desire. It reflected the look in hers. Her body wanted him in a way that surprised her. She ran her hands through his soft, bed messed hair and wrapped her legs around his waist. Demanding him back to her lips before her mind had a chance to talk her out off what she wanted.

Colin growled her name as he traced kisses down her neck. "You make me feel alive and awake in ways that are new to me. I'm not able to resist you." He wrapped his arms around her and his hands found the skin on the small of her back. It was warm and soft. Love poured out of him and planted it on her lips. "You're so beautiful. I want to take you back to bed and spend all day in bed showing you..."

Amanda broke free of his arms and hopped off the counter. With a sheepish smile said, "Come on then. That sounds like an invitation I can't refuse." She hurried down the hall and up the stairs. Colin laughed and followed briskly. He walked into the bedroom to see her standing at the foot of the bed. Her back was turned away from him. Her hair had fallen over her face and he brushed it back to find a shy smile on her lips. "We haven't got all day you know... oh wait, we do. What were you going to show me?" using her finger to gesture him closer.

With that he gently lifted her and placed her on the bed. He pulled his shirt over his head to reveal his sun kissed skin with toned muscles and a patch of light brown hair in the center. Amanda gasped like a school girl seeing a boy shirtless for the first time. She leaned up toward him and kissed his shoulders and ran her fingers through his chest hair. He shuddered at her touch and pulled her to a sitting position. He looked into her eyes as he lifted her shirt over her head. He kissed her shoulder, collar bone and back up her neck. "Ok?"

"I am more than ok. I love your hands on me and I want to put my hands all over you."

"Things like that can go to a man's head." They both laughed and continued exploring each other whispering. The light from the window diminished and turned from gold to orange. Amanda and Colin were tangled in one another's arms and were lacing their fingers together. "Amanda…"

"MMmm…"

"Can we try to keep this going? You are the most remarkable person I have ever met and I want… need you in my life. Please say we can stay like this?"

"Colin… I'm sorry but…" She could feel him hold his breath. "We can't stay like 'this' forever. I need to eat, bathe, and let Toby out and…"

"You are a cruel woman." He said touching her chin with his finger tip.

"I know but I must keep you grounded in reality." She smiled and kissed his hand wrapped in hers. "I would love to stay in your arms, bed, life and heart for as long as you want me. I find you to be the person I never knew I missed."

"Thanks for the reality check. Let's go get a bath and I will feed that beautiful body of yours." He jumped from the bed and offered a hand to take her to the bathroom. "You coming? I need you…" He smiled that sexy grin.

"You need me in the shower?" Amanda raised an eyebrow at him.

"Yes, I need you to wash my back. I can't reach." She took his hand and followed his firm backside into the bathroom laughing.

16

Colin had taken Toby out while Amanda got dressed. They met down in the kitchen. Amanda was looking in the fridge for some cheese to eat with the grapes. Colin walked in the back door and quietly walked up behind her and placed his hands lightly on her hips. "Toby, what's this pretty lady doing in my fridge? Stealing our food?"

Toby barked, causing her to jump and bump her head on the freezer door. "Ouch!" Amanda said rubbing the back of her head. "You're a great protector of cheese Toby but just a false alarm. I plan on sharing what I find in here." She pulled the cheese from the shelf and put it on a cutting board. "Do you like cheese Toby?" Colin handed her a knife and she began cutting then slipping a piece into her mouth before giving one to Toby.

"Wow! You gave him a snack and he was the one who caused you to hit your head. You are one tough…"

"Here, baby." She placed a chunk of cheese to his lips. "Better?"

"Yes. I have been starving and now I will not faint from lack of nourishment. Someone locked me in the bedroom all morning with no food. I was beginning to feel weak." He stood behind her smiling and kissed the nape of her neck. He lifted his lips to her ears and whispered, "You well? Not feeling faint I hope." He now had his hands across her belly, smiling into her hair.

"I was thinking… what that third thing you wanted to ask me was… You invited me here and to your premiere, but there was a third thing you wanted to ask." Turning to face him and resting the cheese next to the grapes.

"Well, I have a confession to make first. I called Steph after we met and asked her some things about you. She gave me some things to think about and I wanted to make sure I had ways to see you again. She told me that you like to write, I had this great plan to ask your help with something… a project of sorts."

"Really… what kind of project?" Amanda was curious now.

"I thought… you might… help me write a screen play for a movie." He looked at his feet, feeling a bit embarrassed.

"I'm flattered, but I have never written anything like that. I have done short stories, but nothing so…"

"Steph sent me one of your stories and I thought it was freaking fantastic. Will you… work with me?"

Amanda stared at the collar of his shirt for a moment, thinking how she could beat Steph. He brushed a finger across her check to bring her back to his plea. "May I think about it?"

"Of course, no pressure. I was inspired and thought we'd make a good team. It would also give us another reason to spend time together."

"You are too cute. Can we sit and eat now? I am feeling… faint." She took a hand to her forehead and pretends to go weak in the knees.

He wrapped an arm around her waist and walked her to the family room to sit on the sofa. They sat and talked and ate for another two hours. Neither one spoke of the fact that Amanda was going home late this afternoon and they were going to be separated for a bit. They were enjoying their time in the moment.

17

Four o'clock was upon them and with it brought a somber mood. Colin quietly rose from napping on the couch to pack and found Amanda had left the house without him knowing. Toby didn't even give her away. He escorted her out to the beach for a walk and was being the ideal guardian for a lone woman on the beach.

Colin used the time in the house to reflect on the weekend and try to make sense of what was happening. He knew that he was falling hard and fast for Amanda. He wasn't sure why or how it all happened but he felt great about her and the time they were having together. *She was strong and didn't need a man to make her feel important or special. She stood out on her own. I really hope the kids like her. Their mother is a wonderful woman but she is different and a breath of fresh air to me.*

He was finished the packing when Toby bounded in the back door. "Hey buddy! Did you have a nice walk?" He said rubbing his head and then belly when Toby crashed onto the floor.

"He is a great partner. You would have been proud of him. He didn't tackle one person this time." Amanda said chuckling. She reached for the water that Colin's hand was offering her. "Thanks."

"Oh, you think he tackles everyone? Oh, no! He only goes after hot girls. I think he is completely smitten with you. There will be no one else for him. You've ruined my dog!" Colin sipped his water trying to hide his laughter.

"I have ruined your dog, huh? Well, here I thought you told him to get me because you were smitten. I was so... wrong...I will have to ..." Colin pressed her against the counter and gently took the bottle from her hand. He kissed her neck and trailed up to her ear and could hear her breath hitch as he moved up.

"Please don't give away my secrets. It worked on you." he whispered into her hair as he lifted her on to the counter.

"What time are we planning on heading back to the city?" She interrupted to keep herself from running upstairs with him. He pulled away from her sensing she was trying to cool things off before they got carried away.

"Will seven be ok?" nibbling on her ears.

"Perfect! Now let me get packed up so I can be ready!" She playfully pushed him away and ran to the bedroom. From upstairs in the hall, she called, "Colin... I could use a little..."

He appeared at the bottom of the stairs smiling that sexy smile, "I thought you'd never ask!"

~e~

Toby was asleep in the back with the bags. The clouds were dancing through the sky and the sun was ducking behind them as they passed. Colin glanced over at Amanda. She was looking out the window but her mind was miles away. "Whatcha thinking about over there?" Colin asked as he gently squeezed her knee. She smiled and wrapped her hand around his. *I can't believe that I feel so deeply for him in such a short time. He was a beautiful man with an ability to wake up so many parts of my soul that had been asleep. How did I get so lucky to meet him and have him in my life?* His eyes were a green that lacked the brightness of before. They reflected the sadness she was feeling. He squeezed her knee again. She leaned over the console and kissed him on the cheek.

"Sorry, just thinking about going home." She sighed.

"Me too. We'll see each other in two weeks when you come up for the premiere? And we can figure out when we can get together after that. I would like to come see you sometime. Would that be ok?"

"Of course! I would love for you to come down. Brett is excited to meet you. We can do all sorts of things. I can show you around."

"I like the sound of that. Could we have some snuggle time too?"

"*You bet!*" She replied laughing at her over-enthusiasm. "May I meet your kids sometime?"

She regretted asking as soon as she did for fear she would scare him. She looked down her hands and pulled her hand from his.

"I would love for you to meet them and...." He reached for her hand. "I know they'll like you and will be happy for us." He pulled her hand to his lips and kissed her fingers. "Now, I will try to cheer up if you will? We will figure it all out. I would rather be happy like we've been all weekend instead of this... melancholy. Ok?"

"Ok." She reached for the radio and found a station that was playing upbeat music. She started tapping her feet and singing.

"I would have thought you had enough of my scary singing." He began dancing and singing from the driver's seat. She smiled at him and nodded. This man was a breath of life awakening Amanda. She was thankful to be with him in this moment listening to him sing off key and dance in his seat. He was being a goof ball and it was absolutely adorable.

18

*B*rett pulled up to the train station and waved to Amanda. He put the car in a space next to the curb. He hopped out and ran to grab his mother's bag. He kissed her cheek, "How was your weekend?" She looked like she got a little more bronze from the sun but there was sadness in her eyes.

"Great. Yours?" She slid into the passenger seat of the car.

"Busy with work but good. I hung out with the guys. I spoke to my roommate and planned to get together with him in a couple of weeks. How's Colin?"

She smiled at Brett for asking about Colin. "He is good. He wants to meet you and hang out with us some weekend before the summer is over. He asked me to write a screenplay with him."

"I'd like to meet him too. Wait….. what…. write a screenplay? That's awesome, Mom. You're a great writer and storyteller. Give me some details." Brett turned Cold Play down to a gentle murmur and waited for more details about the screen play.

Amanda went on to tell him the story behind the screenplay and that Stephanie encouraged Colin to ask. She also explained that

Stephanie shared some of the short stories that she had written. Colin was really keen on it. Brett was asking questions and was impressed that Colin went to such lengths to see his mom again. He must be really into her. They chatted the rest of the ride home.

19

Amanda was spending the day at home catching up cleaning, doing laundry, and trying to keep her mind occupied. She wanted desperately to call Colin, but didn't want to seem like a lovesick teenager. The radio was playing and work was getting done.

Lunch time came around and Amanda was ready to sit out on the deck with her book and enjoy the summer warmth. She grabbed a bottle of water and her book. The lounge chair was in the shade of the umbrella. She pulled the bottom of it into the sun and kept her upper body shaded. The breeze was light and the birds were singing. Laundry was dancing on the line and the neighborhood children were splashing and screaming next door in the pool.

As she began to read, her eyes became heavy and the book fell to her chest. Just as she was relaxing into a nap, Todd sat down beside her.

"Hey Beautiful! How are you today?"

"Todd, what are you doing here?"

"You don't like having me around now that you have Colin?" He said with a smirk.

"No….no. I miss you but it's weird and makes me feel like I am going crazy. Why do you come back to see me?"

"Amanda, I'm glad you're finding happiness." He smiled warmly. "I'm not sure why I can talk to you but I will until I can't anymore."

Amanda hugged herself and looked into his eyes. They were still crystal blue like the Caribbean but something was missing. "What's the matter? You look sad or upset about something."

He squirmed in his seat and looked into her rich brown eyes, so full of life and love. "Honey, I have some things I have to tell you. It's important and I need you to listen until I am finished. Ok?"

Amanda nodded. Her eyebrows furrowed and she scooted to the edge of her seat.

He wanted to put his hands on her knees but figured it wouldn't make a difference in comforting her. "When Brett was 3…"

The doorbell rang and interrupted Amanda from her dream conversation. Her eyes popped open to figure out if the sound was real. It rang again. She jumped off the lounger to get to the door. "I'm coming!" She called as she hastily moved toward the door. Through the window, she could see Mr. Thomas, her lawyer standing next to a young man. She pulled the door open, standing behind the screen door, "Hello, Phil! I didn't expect you today. Everything ok?"

His face was thoughtful with a bit of sadness. "Hi Amanda, honey. I'm sorry to bother you but I need to talk to you right away. May we come in?"

She was feeling uneasy but forced a smile and opened the screen door and invited them in. "Should we go to the kitchen?" leading the way. "Would either of you like something to drink?"

The young man shook his head and Phil replied, "No thank you, dear."

They sat at the table. Phil gave Amanda a sympathetic look. "Phil, you're scaring me. What is this all about?" The young man was sitting at the table looking at his hands and not saying a word. Amanda looked over at him and he must have felt her gaze. He met her eyes and she gasped. *Those were Todd's eyes.*

"Amanda," Phil slid his chair up next to Amanda and covered her hands with his. "Todd wanted me to introduce you to this young man. His name is Michael, and he is Todd's son."

"What.....what? When, how, who?" Amanda stuttered and shook her head. "Brett is his son. We only had one son. He isn't his son. What are you doing here, Phil?" The tone of her voice was turning a bit angrier but tears were running down her cheeks.

The young man, Michael, spoke softly while looking at the table. "My mom and dad met at a convention about 17 years ago. They talked and wrote letters and saw each other when they could. She knew he was married and didn't want to break up his family, but they had an affair and had me. He sent money and took care of both of us for a while. Then it all stopped. I knew where he lived and who you were, so I did some searching online and found out he died." He stopped, took a couple deep breaths, and looked up at Amanda. "I don't want anything from you but I just wanted to find my dad. My mom died last week and I have nowhere to go and no family." His eyes filled with tears and Amanda's heart was breaking for this boy.

Phil looked at both of them and opened his mouth to speak. "Michael's mom had stated in her will that if anything happened to her, Michael was to contact Todd. I have been in contact with her lawyer and we have options."

Amanda's mind was racing. She went back to the conversation she just had with Todd. *This was what he was going to tell me. I can't believe he did this and hid it from me. I trusted him and loved him with all my heart. Now what do I do?* So many emotions were flowing through her. She squeezed Phil's hand and looked at Michael. She pulled her hands from Phil and reached toward Michael. She took her pointer finger to lift his chin. She looked into those beautiful blue eyes and smiled faintly. "You have his eyes." He blinked. "I don't want you to worry but I need some time to process all of this. Phil and I will get it straightened out and you will be cared for, I promise. Do you have a place to stay?"

He nodded and Phil spoke up. "He is staying with my family." Phil's face relaxed a bit and hope was rising in his heart. Todd did a devious thing to both of these people but Amanda was a terrific woman and would make sure this boy doesn't get hurt or lost. She doesn't deserve all of this but she will do what's right and take care of this kid. "Amanda, we can go and talk to you later. Will you call me when you're ready to talk?"

Amanda nodded and stood up from the table. She shook Phil's hand and looked at Michael. She wanted to hug him but wasn't sure if he would welcome that. "Michael, I am sorry for the loss of your mother and father." She patted him the shoulder.

"Thank you."

20

Oh my God! What the hell am I going to do?

Amanda sat at the edge of the grave staring at the headstone. How could she trust and love a man that would have kept this secret from her? Tears were streaming down her face, her phone was buzzing in her pocket. She was numb. She collapsed to the grass, wondering what she was going to do.

How could he do this to us? I thought he was happy and in love with me. Why would he have another family? Was I not good enough? Poor Michael! How can I help him? I know nothing about him. He doesn't know us. He's alone and scared. What the hell am I going to do?

Amanda snapped out of her emotional trace and popped the phone out of her pocket. Two missed calls, Brett. She called back to apologize for not picking up.

"Hey honey! How was work today?" hiding her pain and torment.

"Busy! Where are you?"

"I came to see your dad. You home or out with the guys tonight?"

"Mom, everything ok? Why are you with Dad?"

"Give me fifteen more minutes and I will come home and tell you all about what happened today."

"The guys are just hanging at Scott's place. I'll catch up with them whenever. I'll be here when you get home." Brett was feeling the knot build in his stomach. Amanda rarely went to see Todd so something big must have happened. He wondered if it was something with Colin. He took a couple deep breathes and jumped into the shower.

Brett was sitting in front of the TV when Amanda came home. "I'm down here, Mom!" He called up to her.

"I'll be right down." She replied. While sitting at Todd's grave, she thought more about what she needed to do and how that would impact her life. "Are you eating with the guys, honey?" She called down the stairs.

"Yeah! They're ordering Chinese."

Amanda walked toward the stairs and tried to compose herself. *How am I going to tell Brett that he has a half-brother and his dad had a secret life? What am I going to do? What about Colin and our... whatever it is.*

She plopped on the couch next to Brett. "Whatcha watching?"

"Highlights from soccer, nothing too important. What's up?" He reached for the remote and muted it.

"Phil came to see me today. He needed to tell me some things and introduce me to a young man." Her courage and composure was wavering. "The young man's name is Michael. He just lost his mom. He came here with Phil because..." She started to cry and looked away at the silent soccer game.

"Mom...who's Michael?" Brett felt that knot again and started to slide closer to his mom and put his arm around her.

"It seems that your dad had been taking care of Michael financially for almost fifteen years and was in touch with him and his mother.

Your dad met Michael's mother when you were about three years old and kept in touch. Especially after she became pregnant with Michael, he's your father's son." Amanda watched Brett to see his reaction.

"How did we not know? How could he have lied to us all these years?" Brett felt tightness in his chest and wanted to punch something. "I thought he was a good, honest man. What am I supposed to think now?" He looked at his mother searching for answers.

"Brett…I don't know what to tell you. I'm angry with your father for this deception but I'm sure he had his reasons for lying to us about Michael." She breathed in with tears streaming down her cheeks. "I know that we don't deserve feeling this anger and betrayal. Michael doesn't deserve to be alone without his mother and his father. I loved your dad, but right now I'm pissed at him and don't want to think about him. I want to be selfish and think about what we need and this orphan." She reached for Brett's hand. He pulled her into a hug.

"Mom, I can't believe he did this to us. May I meet Michael?" His eyes were wet with anger and hurt. He broke the hug and rose from the couch. "Did anyone else know?"

"Phil just found out. I don't know if anyone else knew." Amanda stood in front of Brett resting a hand on his forearm. "I need to decide what to do and call Phil. If you want to meet Michael that can happen."

Brett ran his hands through his short hair and over his face. "Thanks. I'd like that. What are you thinking …what are you going to do?"

"I'm not sure but I hope it's the right thing."

"I'm sure you will do the right thing. I'll support whatever you decide." Brett pulled her into another hug. "I love you, Mom."

"I love you too, babe." Amanda squeezed him and smiled warmly into his chest. "I'm very lucky to have you. Thank you for being a wonderful man."

"Thanks for teaching me how to be a good person. I'm sorry Dad did this. We'll get through it. Right now I'm really pissed at him too and I don't want you to be upset with me about that. I don't know how long that will last but I may never forgive him."

"I know you're hurt and I understand completely. Try to forgive him. You don't have to forget but he must've had his reasons. We may never know but we can make the best of what we have." She looked into his eyes and nodded. "You're feelings are entirely justified. Just remember to talk to me if you need to."

"I'm here if you need anything." Brett grabbed his power drink off the coffee table and started toward the stairs. "You ok? I need to get out of my head for a bit."

"Yes, I'll be fine. Go. I'll see you later." She followed him up the stairs and started pulling things out for a sandwich. "Tell the boys hello."

"Will do! I won't be too late." Brett grabbed his keys and ball cap. "Love you!"

"Love you!"

21

*A*manda collapsed on her bed staring at the ceiling. The emotional roller coaster was wearing her out. Yet sleep would not take her. Her brain was racing with thoughts of what to do. *I needed to do something that would be good for Michael and for Brett. How was I going to do it and make everyone happy? What about me and Colin? I wanted happiness too, as selfish as it sounded. Do I have a right to be selfish? What am I going to do about Todd? He royally screwed up and left me in a horrible situation. Why didn't he man up and tell me about his indiscretion? Did he not trust me enough to know I could handle it? I wasn't sure if I would have stayed after finding out about Michael, but it would've been nice to have been given the choice instead of dealing with it after Todd was gone. Dick!* Right now all Amanda wanted to do was scream and throw things at Todd. She had so much that she needed to say to him and no way to do it. She looked up at the spinning ceiling fan and her eyes slowly closed.

"Amanda. I'm so sorry!" Todd pleaded from the end of the bed.

She held up her hand to silence him. "Before you start...I have some things I need to say to you. How could you do this to Brett and

Michael? No boy deserves to be abandoned, lied to, and disregarded by his father. You could have told me and we could have had a relationship with Michael or at the least known he existed, but you denied us the chance until now. Michael didn't know you and Brett knew a man that was an illusion. How can he tell Michael about a dad that he feels like he didn't even know?" Amanda took a deep breath and looked at Todd. His head was hanging low in shame and wringing his hands.

"I can't begin to tell you how sorry I am. I messed up and I should've done all of it differently, but I can't change the mistakes I made. Please know that I was trying to protect all three of you from pain."

"You may be sorry but now I have to fix it and I don't know what to do. This is the biggest thing you have ever asked me to do. How could you leave this to me, Todd?"

"I wish I could help you, Amanda. I didn't mean for you to have to take care of this, but I know you will make a good decision and everyone will be ok." He leaned toward her."

She looked into his eyes. "You hurt me and I'm pissed you. I will do my best but not because of you. I want these two boys to know compassion and love of a family, whether blood or not. I don't know how I will teach that lesson but I'm working on it." She stared at him with hurt in her eyes. "Was this your unfinished business that was keeping you here with me?"

He nodded his head.

"Well, then go. I'll take care of things. I forgive you for the lies and secrets. I will try to remember the good memories of the man that I married." She sobbed and tears were rolling down her cheeks.

"Amanda, I love you and the boys. Please know that I was that man that you married. I just screwed up along the way and let you down. You were the love of my life and unfortunately I was human and betrayed you. I let the boys down. I hope they can learn from my mistakes and be better men. Take care and thank you for picking up the pieces. Good luck with whatever decision you make. It will be a good one." Todd began to walk toward the door and faded to nothing before Amanda broke down completely.

Amanda slept until 2:00 AM and walked to the bathroom to wash the dried tears from her face. She splashed water on her face and toweled herself dry. She had felt better after "talking" to Todd and had come to a decision. She walked back to her bed and picked up her laptop. She opened the email and sent one to Phil before she lost her resolve and explained everything that he needed to know. She typed and tears welled in her eyes, but knew this was the right thing for all people involved.

She reread it to make sure everything was clear and hit send. She breathed out and opened another new message.

> To: Colin
> Subject: Things
> Colin,
>
> Please know that I have loved being with you and getting to know you but I have some things that have come up here at home and I can't see you anymore. This is a horrible way to tell you this and I'm sorry. I suck at good-byes. You're a wonderful man and I fell for you, but I need to focus on some other things right now. Please understand and please don't hate me.
>
> Love,
> Amanda

Again, she reread the message and held her hand to her chest. She didn't want to be selfish. She knew Colin had to be free of her and the drama that was her life. The cursor hovered over the send button, and then she tapped it. Her heart broke as she did it and put her laptop on the bedside table. She reached for the TV remote and pressed the power button. She knew she wouldn't be able to sleep so she watched infomercials until the sun came up. Going for a run was what she needed to help ease her nerves and clear her busy mind. She dressed and walked out into the kitchen to leave a note for Brett.

The morning air was refreshing and the birds were singing a song of a new day. She had made some big decisions early this morning and felt pretty good about one of them. As her run fell into a comfortable rhythm, optimism began to wash over her. It would all be ok.

22

Amanda spent the rest of June and July thinking about Michael and Brett. She remembered what Colin said about writing a screen play and that he thought she was an excellent writer. She thought he was crazy then but an idea had come to her. Amanda was witnessing the changes in both boys and seeing first hand, how life could change overnight.

When she went to bed, she pulled her laptop to her lap and began typing. She had so much "research" material from her daily activities that she was not short on words. The small idea became a big story that took her until July to wrap up. She left the ending open and the future untold. *Why speculate what was going to happen? I wanted to watch and see for myself.*

After agonizing over the words, Amanda sent it to Stephanie to read. She knew that an honest opinion and supportive ideas would be given. It took a week for Stephanie to read it and get back to her.

"Amanda! This is great! I think people will really like this story and want to know what happens to the unlikely family." The pride she felt was coming through her voice. Amanda had been dealing with so much the last six weeks and this must have been therapeutic for her. "May I share it with someone?"

"Oh... no... it isn't good enough for your people." She was nervous and unsure of her writing. She felt bare and naked sharing the story. It felt good to write it down but she didn't want other people to read it?

"The hell it isn't good enough! They're going to *love* it!" Stephanie was trying to ease Amanda with her enthusiasm. "I know exactly who to take it to. Please say I can! *Please!*"

Amanda hesitated and sighed into the phone. "If you think they will like it. Go ahead! You're the expert!"

"Thank you! Thank you! I will make sure they love it!" Stephanie covered the phone and spoke to someone on her end. "Honey, I have to go. Ryan and Sam need to go to practice. I will call you later and let you know what I find out."

"No hurry! I love you, Stephie! Have a good practice. Talk to you later." Amanda hit the end button and returned the phone to the charger. She walked to her room, gathered some laundry and went down stairs to start the washer. She found some more household chores to keep her mind occupied until bedtime. Sleeping had gotten easier since she told Todd to leave her alone. She was lonely but he needed to give her space to clean up his mess. She would always love him but she was still angry with the way he handled the whole situation. It was cowardly. He was a better man than that, Michael and Brett were proof of that.

23

The rest of the summer passed with the speed of light and school started in a week. Amanda hadn't heard from Colin except for a brief email that said he understood and he would miss her. Amanda had spent her summer making sure Michael got settled and Brett got to fulfill his new big brother shoes. Brett and Michael were instant friends. They talked about their memories of Todd and found that the man they both knew was the same. Todd had lied but tried to be a good father to Michael and Brett.

Michael was starting his senior year and Amanda decided to ask him to move into the house with them. She knew that she was not his mother but if he wanted a "step-mother" and a brother, then he was welcome. He helped them make a new family. Michael was thankful and after a few weeks he fell into the harmony of the house. Amanda sighed at how well he fit with them. It had its moments of being weird but they were becoming a family and the decision to invite him was the best one Amanda could have made.

Stephanie called once a week and checked on all of them and she even brought the kids to house. Brett and Michael were great with her little angels. They played in the yard and watched movies. The Saturday before school was set to start; Stephanie was there for a visit. All the kids were running around the yard with water guns of all shapes and sizes. Stephanie and Amanda were sipping sangria on the deck.

"How did we do without Michael before? He brings Brett out of his shell and completes this family in a great way." Stephanie grinned and held Amanda's hand.

"I'm so glad we found each other. It could have turned out so much worse. They are both great boys and I'm so thankful that Phil helped him find us. I just hope that he feels the same way about us." She looked over at Stephanie with a brief look of worry in her eyes. Just then a stream of water shot at the two moms sitting together. There were screams of shock and giggles followed. All four boys were hiding behind the tree trying not to be seen. Amanda reached under the chair for the hidden water gun and fired back in retaliation. The smallest boys squealed and ran. The two big boys laughed and chased them squirting at them.

"I think Michael loves you guys too. Does he talk about his mom much?" Stephanie chuckled.

"He does. She sounded like a pretty amazing mom. He brought his furniture from his house and lots of pictures. From what he has told me and the pictures I have seen, I understand why Todd fell for her. I wish that I could've met her. I think we would have been friends. I hope that she approves of what we're doing for Michael."

"I'm sure she's grateful for the role you have taken in his life."

The evening continued with dinner and getting the young boys into bed. Brett and Michael went to a movie with friends, one last time before school started. The house was still and quiet around nine o'clock and Stephanie and Amanda were setting out back again enjoying the light show from the fireflies.

"You know he asks about you all the time?"

"Who?"

"Colin, silly woman! I explained to him what happened and told him what you were doing. He's really proud of the choice you made. He misses you but knows the boys needed to be your priority." Stephanie turned toward Amanda and looked into her eyes. "You can be selfish now!"

"What? Colin doesn't need this." She said motioning to the house and herself. "I miss him too, but I don't want to put one more thing on his already full plate." She frowned.

"Honey, he'd say if he couldn't handle all this. He fell hard for you and wants to be with you, all of you." Stephanie hugged Amanda and stood. "Think about it. Good night, sweetie!" She walked into the house and down to the basement.

Amanda sat for a few more minutes and went to bed too. She ached for Colin but was afraid that her life was too much for him. She didn't want to ask him to be part of her mess.

She got ready for bed and heard a light tap on the door. "Amanda… we're home."

"Come in Michael." She smiled as he peeked in the doorway. "Thanks for letting me know. Did you have fun tonight?"

"The guys are great! I didn't have many friends at home since I helped to take care of Mom, so it's nice to hang out with guys and just be one of the gang. That sounded stupid didn't it? I hope they don't think I'm as uncool as I sound." Michael looked down at his shoes unsure of himself and his honesty.

"I'm sure they all think you're cool. Don't worry! I know exactly what you mean about just being with friends. Stephanie makes me feel that way too. Michael, may I ask you something?" Amanda walked toward the door and looked into his young, innocent eyes. She saw him nod and then asked, "Are you glad you're here? We are so glad that you decided to stay with us and be part of our little family."

Michael looked down at his shoes again and took a breath. He looked back into Amanda's eyes. His misty eyes reflected her emotion. "I miss my mom but I'm glad to be with you and Brett. You both make me feel not so lonely. Thanks for making the offer. I'm glad to be part of this family." He stepped toward Amanda and pulled her into a hug.

"You too ok?" Brett emerged from the bathroom to see them hugging.

They both replied, "Yeah!" They both looked at each other and then Brett and pulled him into the hug.

"You two are weird!" He said wiggling out of their hug. "But thanks for the hug. Good night!"

"Good night boys! See you in the morning!" Amanda chuckled and backed away from the door.

"Night, Amanda!"

24

*A*manda was tired and snuggled under the sheet. Finally she felt like she could sleep peacefully. The house was quiet and the boys were home safe. Her eyes grew heavy as soon as she laid her head on her pillow. Sleep crept up on her quickly. Her body relaxed and welcomed the rest. Her mind had been so busy for so many weeks that relief was exuding from every pore.

Amanda heard a whisper in her ear. It was Todd's voice.

"Amanda, you're doing a wonderful thing for both Brett and Michael. Thank you for taking care of these great young men. I know that you don't want to see me but I needed to tell you something. You need to do something for yourself now. You took care of the boys but it's your turn. Take care of you. I love you and you deserve to have Colin in your life. He loves you and you love him. Go to him or call him. Be happy. Good night sweetheart! Sweet dreams!"

Amanda rolled onto her back. Her eyes fluttered. "Goodbye Todd. Thank you for giving me two great boys." She continued dreaming.

25

The morning light poured into the room and kissed Amanda's cheek. She woke with in a cheerful mood and an idea for what she was going to do for the day. It was her last Sunday before school started. Stephanie and the kids would be going home today and Brett would be working. Michael would be chilling before his senior year started tomorrow. She reached for her laptop and began an email.

To: Colin
Subject: Question
Colin,

Hello! How are you? I hope this note finds you well. How are the kids and Toby? I hope they had a great summer. Sorry I missed the premiere and the beach house. I know that you have spoken to Stephanie and know what has been going on with me. I've been thinking about you and didn't want to bother you with all of my drama, but I miss you. I completely

understand if you don't want to get involved in this
mess. I just wanted to say that I miss you and I still
have feelings for you.

Please let me know if you feel the same way and are
willing to work on us.

I hope to hear from you soon.

Love,
Amanda

Amanda read over her note and hit send without thinking twice.
She knew that she owed Colin a chance. He was a good man that she
was crazy about but she also didn't want to overwhelm him with her
new situation. She closed her eyes and thought to herself. *No matter
what he decides, all I can do is be honest and tell him how I feel. If he doesn't
feel the same, then I tried. That was all I could do.*

It was nine o'clock when Amanda finally put her laptop away and
threw some clothes on before going out to the kitchen. Stephanie and
her boys were carrying their bags to the front door. Amanda stopped
and looked at them with confusion. "Where are you guys going?"

"Aunt Amanda… we're going for breakfast and getting on the
train. Daddy called and said we needed to come home." Ryan looked
just like his daddy.

"Is everything ok?" Amanda asked looking at Stephanie with
worry.

"Yes, dear! Everything's fine. Doug got a call from the office to
go out of town, but wanted to see us before he leaves. We got packed
and Brett and Mike offered to take us to the train station." Steph
answered with humor in her voice. "You worry too much!"

"Sorry! I thought you guys would be here for lunch and we could get more time together." She had a hint of sadness in her voice. Brett came bounding in the door.

"Ready guys?" He grabbed Ryan and Sam's bags and headed back out to the car. Ryan and Sam ran to Amanda.

"Bye Aunt Amanda! Thanks for a fun weekend!" They sang in unison as they hugged her goodbye and ran to the car. Michael scooped them up and whisked them into the back seat.

"Did you think more about what I said last night? I was just trying to help and be supportive. I love you sweetie!" As Stephanie hugged Amanda, "Thanks for the get-away. We love coming down to visit you three. I'll call when we get home, ok?"

Amanda smiled and hugged her back. She sighed into her hair and replied, "Yes, I thought about what you said and I'm glad you'll tell me what I need to hear whether I want to or not. I love you too. Please call me so I know you made it." The girls laughed and Amanda watched her walk out to the car. Michael was in the back seat with the boys and Brett was putting Stephanie's bag in the trunk. Everyone waved as the car pulled away from the house. Amanda stood and watched the car disappear down the road. She hugged herself and walked back inside.

Amanda went down stairs and started taking sheets of the inflatable mattress and sofa bed. As the inflatable mattress was deflating, she tucked the sleeper back into the sofa. The mattress got rolled and tucked into the storage bag. Amanda finished putting the room back in order and carried the sheets to the laundry room. *I can hang those out later.* She thought to herself.

DING DONG the doorbell chimed from upstairs. "What did you forget?" She said hurriedly opening the door. It wasn't Stephanie. "Hello! What are you doing here?" She smiled awkwardly.

"I have a delivery." He stood holding stack of papers bound

together. Amanda could see the words *Unlikely Family* on the black cover.

"What's that?" Amanda couldn't keep the confusion from her voice and face. Her eyebrows drew closer on her forehead.

"Well… a friend of mine…ours…gave me this screenplay about a month ago and I needed to know how it ends." He held out the screenplay to her. "I just got the green light to find the people to make it happen. I thought the writer should know that her work is amazing. I wanted to deliver the message personally. I figured it would be ok because…well… I … I did get an email this morning from her."

Amanda smiled and nodded. Her voice was choked in her throat and tears were threatening to escape her eyes.

Colin continued, "She asked me if I still felt the same, so I'm here to say I want to be part of her story. She is a beautiful woman and I love her. I wanted to tell her that I want her and her sons. She is the best thing that has happened to me in a long time and I have missed her terribly for the past two months."

"I see." Amanda smiled and winked at him. "You can come in." Amanda opened the screen door. Colin walked in and lifted her off her feet into a tight, passionate hug. The kiss that followed made her weak in the knees and thankful for him holding her so tightly. "I missed you too! I'm so sorry I had to be away from you."

"Promise me that we don't need to do that again. I know our kids are important to us and that we are used to handling things on our own, but let's do it together from now on." Colin looked into her eyes with so much love. He leaned in to kiss her nose and rested his forehead on hers. "I want to be part of your happy ending."

"Who knows what tomorrow will bring, but we will see it together."